THE OFF SEASON

THE OFF SEASON

by

Catherine Gilbert Murdock

Houghton Mifflin Company

Boston 2007

www.houghtonmifflinbooks.com

The text of this book is set in Dante.

Library of Congress Cataloging-in-Publication Data

Murdock, Catherine Gilbert.
The off season / by Catherine Gilbert Murdock.
p. cm.
Summary: High school junior D.J. staggers under the weight of caring
for her badly injured brother, her responsibilities on the dairy farm,
a changing relationship with her friend Brian, and her own athletic
aspirations.
ISBN-13: 978-0-618-68695-7 (hardcover)
ISBN-10: 0-618-68695-9 (hardcover)
[1. Football—Fiction. 2. Interpersonal relations—Fiction. 3. Farm life—
Fiction.] I. Title.
PZ7.M9415Off 2007
[Fic]—dc22
2006029278

Manufactured in the United States of America
QUM 10 9 8 7 6 5 4 3 2 1

To Mimi and Nick,
for their many excellent suggestions

Contents

THE OFF SEASON

1

THE JORGENSENS' LABOR DAY PICNIC

EVERY LABOR DAY, the Jorgensens — they own Jorgensens' Ice Cream — set up a little ice cream stand right in their yard, which means you can spend the entire Labor Day picnic making yourself ice cream sundaes if that's what you want to do, and for years when I wasn't playing softball or chasing the Jorgensen kids or trying to keep up with my brothers, I'd sit myself at that little booth making one sundae after another until it was time to head home for evening milking, and then a couple miles into the drive I'd bring that whole sundae experience back up, right there on the side of whatever road we happened to make it to. Lately, though, I have a little more self-control. Now I only eat three or four, without marshmallows because I finally figured out that they shouldn't really be part of the whole sundae thing, while I'm hanging out at the pig roast watching guys poke at the fire because apparently it's a law that if you're a guy you have to spend a bunch of time doing that. Then maybe I'll grab one more between innings when I'm not pitching.

That's the other great thing about the picnic: the softball

game. Randy Jorgensen has a huge backyard he mows all year for this, and he borrows bases from Little League so it's official and all. He even got an umpire's getup at a garage sale somewhere, and a friend of his who owns a pig farm works every year as umpire after he's got the pig going in the pit.

My mom used to pitch the game. She pitched all through college, and her team was pretty good from what she's told me. Then one year she threw her back out, which isn't that hard to believe considering she doesn't get much exercise these days and, well, she weighs a whole lot more than she used to. She threw out her back so much that she couldn't walk or anything, Dad had to drive her home in the back of the pickup as she lay there like a piece of plywood if plywood could holler to slow down, and she had to spend three weeks on the living room floor until she healed. Which isn't such a swell thing to be doing when you're supposed to be teaching sixth grade and it's the first three weeks of school.

So she's not allowed to pitch anymore. But at least she started exercising again—not for softball but just to lose some weight—which means puffing around the farm fields, swinging her arms in this way that makes me glad she's not walking where anyone can see her. I guess she figures that an elementary school principal, which she is now since she moved up from teaching sixth grade, shouldn't be quite so heavy.

The softball game is always kids against the grownups,

from little tiny kids still in diapers to old farmers who get their grandkids to run because they don't have any knees left. There's always lots of arguing about where the teenagers should go. This year Randy Jorgensen made a big plea for Curtis, trying to get him on the grownup side on the grounds that he's one of the tallest people there, which is true, but seeing as he's only going into eighth grade he really does belong on the kids' team.

After Mom hurt her back, Randy tried pitching but he took it way too seriously, and the next year Mom suggested me, and now I guess it's just tradition. Which is nice because I don't play school softball seeing as I run track, and this fall of course I was playing football, which is another whole story in and of itself, so this is how I get my softball fix. Plus I'm not too biased. Mom says I'm Switzerland, which I think she means as a compliment.

Besides, it's not like competitive softball. You mostly just try to get the ball across the plate slow enough for whoever's trying to hit it, and keep it dry from the guys who hit with a beer in their other hand. Some little kids hold the bat out like they've never held a bat before, which some of them haven't, and I'll toss the ball as gently as I can against the bat, which in this game counts as a hit, and the kid will be so surprised they'll just stand there while everyone starts hollering, and their mom will have to take them by the hand to run around the bases, and in the meantime the catcher, who's usually

Randy's wife, Cindy, will toss to first but just happen to over-throw, and so the kid will continue on to second just totally amazed, and the second baseman will fumble eight or nine times with a bunch of moaning, and the kid will make it to *third*, and sometimes if there are enough errors the kid will score a home run and walk around on a cloud for the rest of the afternoon.

With other folks, of course, I'm not so nice. Mom always takes a couple turns at bat even though she shouldn't be-cause of her back. All the younger kids in the outfield think this is hilarious, their principal standing there in her big floral shorts and her big pink T-shirt, looking a lot more like a beach ball than a batter. But the older kids know enough to back up. One year she hit the ball so hard it took twenty min-utes to find it. I guess she needs to get her softball fix in too, and also needs to teach those kids a lesson or two about mouthing off.

Then there's Curtis, who's always a huge part of the game, and I'm not just talking about his playing. My little brother might not talk to grownups much, or to me, but with little kids he's just amazing. I don't know if it's because they can tell, the way dogs can sometimes, that he's safe and he'll be really nice to them, which he will. Or maybe he's just a lot more comfortable with kids than older folks, and they pick up on that. But wherever he goes where there are little kids, like this picnic, they just flock to him. As soon as Curtis and this girl he was hanging out with sat down on the edge of the softball field, a half-dozen little kids started climbing on him and giggling and asking him questions, and he settled into it like being a human playground was his calling in life. Whenever the littlest kids went up to bat, he'd run the bases with them if they wanted, and in the outfield he'd make sure they got to tag out their dads and uncles, who often tripped really dramatically right before the base so it'd be easier for the kids to get them.

And then when it was Curtis's turn to hit, the kids got so excited they were just exploding. Curtis after all was a state MVP in Little League, which everyone in town knows including the dead people, and when he walked up to home plate, the kids started zipping like bugs around a porch light, and all the folks in the outfield went *way* back, knowing what was coming, and I switched from nice-girl-tossing-the-ball-against-the-bat to big-sister-you-can-eat-this-one mode.

I pitched a fast one and Curtis swished a strike, and the little kids went bonkers like this was the World Series or something, and then he smashed right through my second pitch and it was clear that all those folks in the outfield hadn't gone back nearly far enough, and he ambled off toward first base because that ball was a couple hours from being found.

A bunch of little kids, though, took that ambling personally. They ran up and started tugging on his arms, and his legs even, shrieking at him to run, and then another bunch of kids, his defenders, decided that this first group shouldn't be so bossy and so they started pulling Curtis the other way because I guess they decided that walking would make him happier. Until finally you couldn't even really see Curtis, just a dozen little kids hollering and waving their arms and giggling hysterically, pulling him in every direction.

You know the expression "fall down laughing"? I actually did. I was laughing so hard, standing there on my little pitcher's mound, that after a while my knees didn't work and I had to lie down and try to breathe as I watched Curtis getting dragged around the bases. It was, hands down, the funniest thing I've ever seen.

Anyway, that's a very long story that doesn't have much to do with anything. But even now that memory makes me grin, Curtis and all those little kids wriggling together . . . It's hard to believe, sitting here in the hospital writing this down, that I ever felt so happy. That once, not so long ago, my life actually seemed okay.

2

An Extra Hand at Evening Milking

One of the annoying things about dairy farming—I
mean, there are a ton of annoying things, like the smell, although you get used to that pretty quick, and the fact you
spend your so-called summer vacation bringing in hay and
worrying about the weather, and that Dad never spends any
money to fix anything so all our equipment is just a hair from
being completely broken—but one of the most annoying
things is that you have to milk the cows twice a day no matter what. It's not like you can take a day off and go somewhere and they'll milk themselves. You have to be there
every morning and every night. If you're even a couple hours
late, their udders get too full of milk and the cows can get
really sick. Which is why we had to leave the Labor Day picnic after only five innings. Although one nice thing is that the
Jorgensens are friends with a bunch of dairy farmers so it's
not like we were the only ones skipping out early. Randy and
Cindy are pretty used to it.

Anyway, we were still pretty late getting home, which the
cows weren't too shy about telling us, and even from inside

the Caravan I could hear them mooing up a racket when we pulled in. I was so busy watching the cows push against the gate to get milked and figuring that I should probably offer to help Dad before he flat-out told me to that I didn't even look toward the house, which is why when Mom said, "Isn't that Brian?" my heart stopped for a second.

You see, our world of cows and busted equipment and twice-a-day milking doesn't have one thing to do with the other world — the real world, I think of it — of normal families and popular girls and good looks and Brian Nelson. There wasn't a reason I could think of for him to be sitting on our kitchen step with school starting the next morning, plus the cows making a racket and Smut wagging her tail all over the place and practically crawling into his lap, she was so glad to see him. But there he was.

"Hey there, Mr. Schwenk, Mrs. Schwenk," he called out with his nice manners as we piled out of the Caravan.

"Hey there, Brian," said Dad. "Whatcha doing here?"

Brian shrugged. "Just passing by." Which was impossible because our farm is something you pass only if you're headed to nowhere. "Hey, Curtis."

Curtis hunched down, staring at the ground. "Hey," he whispered, his ears bright red. Like I said, Curtis isn't so great with anyone over the age of ten. Or eleven, maybe.

"You gonna give us a hand with the milking?" Dad asked Brian in that way he has.

"You don't have to —" I started to say really fast, but Brian just shrugged again.

"Sure." He came over to the back of the Caravan, where Mom was unloading the buckets of food we hadn't eaten and our lawn chairs from the softball game.

"Hey, D.J.," he murmured, coming up beside me to take a load.

"Hey," I said, wishing like anything that my ears weren't turning bright red too. "How's your arm feel?" I asked. Quarterbacking an entire game, which is what he'd done Friday for the Red Bend–Hawley scrimmage, can really wear you down.

"Not bad," he said, swinging it a little. "How about your ribs?" During the scrimmage a couple Hawley players had kicked me pretty hard. That sort of roughing up comes with the territory in football, especially when you've got two teams that hate each other as much as Red Bend and Hawley. *Especially* when you happen to be a girl playing varsity in her very first game, a girl with two older brothers who are pretty much football legends around our two towns.

I shrugged. "Okay. The bruising's fading." I said this kind of quietly because I didn't want Mom hearing I even had rib bruises and getting all fluttery on me. Besides, it wasn't Brian's fault that so many other Hawley guys were jerks.

After we'd unloaded the Caravan, Brian came right into the barn with me and Curtis and Dad, helping put the feed out, which goes super fast with four people, and opening the doors so the cows could go to their places they all have memorized, the cows so happy to be eating grain and getting milked at last.

Dad was in a pretty good mood—he'd had a couple beers at the Jorgensens', and it's always a boost to have extra hands with milking—and he kept chattering away about the picnic, how Brian should have been there to see Curtis and me play. Brian shot me a look, and we grinned at each other because Dad can be a little over the top. If I didn't know Brian so well, I'd be just about dying. But it was okay.

"You should come with us next year," Dad offered, like the only thing Brian would want to do on Labor Day was play softball with a bunch of smalltime farmers and ice cream store folks from Red Bend when he could be off doing something much cooler with the kind of pretty girl that guys like Brian date.

"Sorry, but I'll be at college," Brian said, sounding sorry even.

"That's right, isn't it. Gonna play college ball?"

"I hope to. Sir."

Which got everyone on a discussion of Win and Bill, my two big brothers, and the University of Washington and the University of Minnesota, how those two teams were going to do and how much better both of those teams were—how much better both *schools* were, from the way Dad talked—with Schwenks playing football for them.

Through all this talk, I couldn't help thinking how nice it would have been to have Brian at the Jorgensens' picnic, poking at the pig roast and talking football and playing in the game. Maybe if he wasn't from Hawley. Or maybe if he was from Hawley but I was a normal girl so you could see why he'd be hanging out with me. Not that we were Officially Dating or anything like that, although we'd talked about it a little, and we'd even tried making out once, in such an awful way that I still winced thinking about it. I mean, Brian had tried to make out with me but I didn't figure out what was going on and ended up giving him a bloody nose. Which is a pretty good way to make sure you *never* date a guy, I think, doing that.

Also, having Brian at the picnic would have been especially awkward given that pretty much everyone there had been at the scrimmage, and all afternoon whenever I wasn't pitching, folks would come up to tell me how well I'd played, how I looked almost like Bill out there on the field, and how great my interception of Brian had been. Which probably wouldn't have made Brian's day, hearing that, even if I was probably the first girl linebacker to score in the whole history of Wisconsin, which several folks had to tell me. Plus that scrimmage was the first time in four years that Red Bend had beaten Hawley in football, so it mattered a lot to everyone in Red Bend, and three days later at the picnic they were still celebrating. Even when I was eating ice cream, I'd get slapped on the back and stuff. I tried to act like the guys on

TV, saying it was all teamwork and the season hadn't even started. Which is something you never see on TV, guys being forced to talk with their mouths all full of vanilla ice cream and chocolate sauce and walnuts. And chocolate on their chins too, probably, if it was me on TV.

Still, it was great having Brian giving us an extra hand with evening milking, the barn still fresh with that new paint the two of us had slapped up, and him finally looking comfortable with our big, big cows. He sure hadn't been comfortable with them at the beginning of the summer, but then, he hadn't been comfortable with any of us. It's not exactly Disney World when your coach sends you off to a rundown old farm because he doesn't think you have a work ethic. By the looks of it, though, Brian sure had found one, because he sure seemed to like hanging around us now.

As we were finishing up, Dad asked Brian if he'd like to stay for dinner. We'd already eaten a ton of food but I was starving again, go figure, and I guess Dad was too. Plus Mom had brought home a big chunk of meat from the pig roast that made me twice as hungry, remembering that.

Brian checked his watch. "Aw, I should go home. You know, first day of school and all." He sounded really nice when he said it, like he wished he didn't have to.

I walked him out to his Cherokee.

"So there, did you have a nice Labor Day?" I asked, doing my best imitation of Mom.

Brian laughed. "I just hung out with some guys. We didn't do anything as fun as that softball game. That would have been a blast."

That was so great, hearing that. "Yeah, well, you can come next year," I said. "Skip college, come play softball instead."

"Don't tempt me." He grinned at me. There was this little pause, and I wondered what was going to happen. The last time we'd been together, Brian had kissed my forehead. It had been really nice, actually, not bloody or embarrassing at all. This time, however, we sort of shuffled a little, and he climbed into the Cherokee still grinning. "I didn't know you were a pitcher too. You're good at everything, aren't you?"

And then he left before I had time to come up with an answer, an explanation about how I'm not good at most things, it's only with sports and cows that I can even pretend to be okay. I stood there in the yard for some time watching the dust settle back down to earth from the Cherokee, enjoying his compliment so much even if it wasn't true, and thinking how much I liked Brian Nelson.

3

FOOTBALL AND BARBECUE

NORMALLY IN SCHOOL I'm one of those invisible people who the cool kids don't notice and the jerks don't pay attention to because I'm too big to pick on, and it's just me hanging out with Amber. Only Amber wasn't there Tuesday morning for the first day of school. Which really freaked me out, and made walking the halls even harder because now I didn't have anyone to talk to while bunches of people—and I mean bunches—kept looking at me. All because I was playing football. Kids slapped me on the back, saying hello, which wasn't bad or anything but sure wasn't something I was used to.

Even this little freshman whose locker was next to mine kept staring at me as he tried to open his combination.

"Hey," I said. To be friendly and all.

The poor kid nearly jumped out of his skin at the sound of my voice.

"Want some help?" I offered, because he was really struggling.

He shook his head. There are times when I'm next to

someone and I don't feel incredibly taller than that person, and bigger too. This was not one of those times.

"I'm D.J.," I said, taping up pictures of Win and Bill in their college uniforms, and Smut wagging her tail off with her slimy old football.

"I know," he said, sounding kind of like a mouse. Kind of squeaky. At least he got his locker open finally. "I'm Paul Zorn."

"Pleased to meet you," I said. I slammed my locker shut the way you do.

Paul jumped again at this noise, then apologized for jumping. Oh boy. "Hey," he managed to squeak out as I walked away. "Good game!"

That was what the first day of school was like for me.

My favorite class, I knew already, was going to be anatomy and physiology. Mr. Larson is one of the coolest teachers in Red Bend. Even Bill, who in a perfect world would play football three hours a day and spend the other twenty-one drinking beer with pretty girls, he liked Mr. Larson. When Mr. Larson isn't teaching A&P, or physics, which only the smart kids take and which no one named Schwenk has ever signed up for, he's enforcing the rules. In the fall he's a football ref, in the winter he's a basketball ref, and in the spring he's a baseball umpire. In the summer, I don't know, maybe he's a lifeguard. This means that in class whenever he's explaining something really complicated, he's got a great sports analogy to make it understandable, and whenever he needs to describe some horrifically disgusting injury, he has a real-life example. Like when he was talking about knees and he brought in a guy who'd been illegally clipped — the guy had a cane and everything — to illustrate it.

Plus I had English with Mrs. Stolze again — but not sophomore English, which was a really good sign because it meant that maybe she'd actually passed me — and Spanish, and algebra, and world history with a textbook that was written back before there was even a United States, it looked like, and a health class you can sleep through, and computers. Which was good because our computer is so old that it's a wonder it even works off electricity. It should use coal, or a little treadmill a goat walks on. One of my ancestors invented that for churning butter — we've even got a picture — although it probably didn't work any better than most of Dad's inventions. So anything related to computers was something I needed to know.

All day long kids kept talking to me about the scrimmage like I was some sort of public property that anyone could just walk right up to. Which I didn't care for much. I mean, I didn't set out to play football because I wanted lots of attention, I was doing it — well, I was doing it because for a while last summer, I wasn't sure what the whole point of life was, and trying out for the football team was the best way I could think of to prove to myself that I was alive and, you know, a unique individual, not just a cow doing what I was told. Only it's not like I could ever explain that to anyone, and certainly not in the hallways of Red Bend High School. Or in the locker room after school either, when I was suiting up for football with all the volleyball players glaring at me and not so curious about my cow worries because they were too busy being mad that I quit volleyball for football, and because of me Kari Jorgensen quit volleyball for cheerleading, and then Amber quit to work at the Super Saver, so the volleyball team was now worse than ever.

Luckily once I got to football practice there wasn't any time to think. From the way Jeff Peterson acted, you'd think we'd lost that scrimmage by thirty-five points instead of winning like we did, and he put us through some kind of workout.

By the time we headed home, I was just beat. Plus I had a ton of homework already. It was like, boom, yesterday was summer and today I was up to my neck in work. Curtis was just as beat from his football practice, although he spent the whole ride reading my A&P book, probably the section on teeth considering he secretly wants to be a dentist. Even Mom seemed fried. I guess being principal can be just as tough as being a kid.

Right as we walked into the kitchen, though, the phone was ringing, and Dad hollered that someone better pick it up, and it was Brian, and all of a sudden my exhaustion evaporated like sweat. I took the portable phone into the little office, which is as far as you can go with our phone because it's so old. "Hey, how are ya?"

I could hear Brian smiling through the phone. I'm sure that seems impossible, but I know what his smile sounds like. "Not so bad . . . How was your first day?"

"Oh, awesome," I lied, and we laughed. Oh, man, did it feel good to talk to him.

We chatted about classes for a bit, and then Brian said like he couldn't wait any longer: "Hey, there's this truck part my dad needs in Minneapolis, and he wants me to go pick it up on Saturday morning. You wanna come with me?"

I couldn't believe it — a road trip to *Minneapolis* with *Brian.*

"My mom wants me to go with someone," he added, "and she figures you're, you know, safer than some of my friends."

Smart woman. I wouldn't trust Brian's Hawley friends with a broken tractor. "Sure!" I managed to say finally. "That would be awesome."

"That's great. I'll pick you up around ten, I figure —"

"Oh no, wait." *Saturday.* Saturday, if you don't know, is college football day, every weekend all fall, and both my brothers were playing on national television. That is, Win, my oldest brother, was a backup QB, which meant he could go in at any moment, and Bill they were talking about starting even though he's only a sophomore. I couldn't give that up, even for a trip to Minneapolis with Brian. Sure, we tape the games with our dusty old VCR but you can't watch the tape. Well, you can, later. But you have to watch the game exactly while it's happening because . . . Well, I can't explain. You just do.

"I'm sorry, it's just the Saturday games—"

"Aw, jeez! I should have remembered. I didn't even think—"

"It's okay. Maybe some other time." Boy, did I hate saying those words. I mean, if there was some way to do both things . . . but no. So we talked another minute, and then I went to dinner feeling like a bug that had run into a windshield, just in time for Dad to serve this thing with goat cheese, which tastes extremely weird if you've never had it before.

About ten minutes later, though, Brian called again. "Hey, guess what! We can go Sunday instead. I mean, if you can make it."

So I asked Mom and Dad, and of course they couldn't say yes right away because they had to go into all these extremely embarrassing questions about where we were going and how long we'd be gone and when we'd be back, and what kind of driver Brian was, like I had his record in front of me, and Mom had to point out I hadn't been to church in a while, like that would be a deal breaker, but finally they said okay, and I got to tell Brian okay and get off the phone before Dad got too much grumpier about his goat cheese getting all cold, and let me tell you, that goat cheese tasted a heck of a lot better, and everything else as well, now that I was going to get to go on a road trip with Brian Nelson.

Wednesday, Amber came to school at least, with all these stories about driving to St. Paul with Dale and insisting I hang out with her and Dale on Saturday night. Which gave me something to think about you can bet, given that Dale is, well, I guess you could say that she's Amber's girlfriend although Amber didn't actually use that word and you can be sure I didn't. Then after practice Jeff announced that I had officially passed sophomore English, which meant I could officially play football, and from the way the guys cheered, I felt more than ever like I was part of the team. That was the other second-day-of-school news.

Friday night we played Cougar Lake, which is always a tough game because we're so evenly matched. Not to mention the Cougar Lake players, and some fans it sounded like, didn't care one bit that there were TV cameras filming the game, and a bunch more spectators than normal, so long as they could kill that girl from Red Bend. After those first couple tackles, I fought back as much as I could, and whenever I played offense I'd stay really close to Kyle Jorgensen because the refs always keep an eye out for the QB. At one point this Cougar Lake guard even grabbed my face mask, which is extremely illegal, and Cougar Lake lost fifteen yards and we ended up scoring, which Jeff Peterson couldn't help pointing out is what happens when you lose your temper and he was sure none of us would be so stupid. We ended up winning 24–16, which was pretty great, and during that whole game I only thought about Brian and Minneapolis three times. Maybe four.

Saturday morning, even though I was so sore I could barely move, I still had to help Dad and Curtis get the first of the silage in, and the last of the alfalfa, the three of us working like dogs, even Mom lending a hand though she's not supposed to be lifting bales, so we'd be ready when Jimmy and Kathy Ott came over to watch the games.

The Otts come to watch every game they can at our house, or we go to theirs, because they're as much a part of our crazy football family as, well, as me, when I think about it. Actually, it's pretty funny that we're all so close given that Jimmy Ott coaches the Hawley football team and he spent a bunch of years training his players to beat the stuffing out of Win and Bill, and now he's training them to beat the stuffing out of me. But because of all that stuffing training, I guess, or because he and Dad are such good friends, and Mom and Kathy are too, the Otts care about Win and Bill playing just as much as we do, and Jimmy follows their games so closely that you'd think he was their personal coach. Plus it was Jimmy's idea to send Brian over here to work for us in the first place because he's the number one fan of the Schwenk

Work Ethic. So if nothing else, I'll always be grateful to him for that.

Bill started! They said his name right there in the opening lineup, that he was a sophomore from Wisconsin and grew up on a dairy farm and his older brother plays for Washington. Oh, that was *so* awesome, and I was so glad I was sitting in our living room with my family and my parents' best friends rather than driving to Minneapolis, even with Brian. Minnesota lost, but Bill played really well, although it's hard to tell because all the camera ever does is follow the ball, which a linebacker doesn't spend too much time with. But Bill had some great tackles that we could see, and if nothing else he didn't embarrass himself, which some days is the most you can hope for.

Right after Bill's game ended, Washington was on another network. For some guys, backup QB would be the most frustrating thing in the world because in four years of college you might not play fifteen minutes. But Win is so serious about football that it didn't matter, because he works so hard and gets everyone else working so hard that he's absolutely critical to the team. And let me tell you, if I had Win right behind me breathing over my shoulder, I'd work my butt off trying to stay ahead of him. And the impression I got from Win was that Washington's starting quarterback felt exactly the same way.

But here's the thing: five minutes into the second quarter,

the starting QB took a bad sack and had to be pulled out. So right there before our eyes Win ran in, the announcer mentioning how he grew up on a dairy farm in Wisconsin and has a younger brother who plays for Minnesota. Which we already knew from the previous game.

Actually, it was pretty frustrating because the phone kept ringing with neighbors congratulating us and making sure we were watching, letting us know they were taping it too. I was so busy being polite I missed this pass Win threw, a good thirty-six yards right to his receiver, but they replayed it about six times, and the touchdown that came from it. And right near the end of the game, Win scored a touchdown from the eleven-yard line and the announcers couldn't stop saying how good Washington's backup quarterback was.

By the time that game was over, *all* of us had to help with the milking, we were so late. Even Jimmy came out to rehash it with Dad as we worked. Curtis joined in a couple times with these little observations that catch you totally off-guard, like how Win spun to the right before he ran to make it look like he'd be passing instead, which I hadn't even noticed and now I had to look at Curtis twice, trying to figure out what made him so smart.

Halfway through milking, Mom came trotting out to say Win was on the phone, which is a very big deal because Dad and Win hadn't talked since December. I got to the kitchen in time to hear Dad tell Win how proud he was, and get all .

choked up and have to blow his nose. That was pretty great—not the nose-blowing part, but the rest of it. I had to blow my nose too.

So all in all it was a pretty big Saturday, and it wasn't until I was in the shower getting ready to go to Amber's that I had the time to wonder about this Dale person. I mean, I'd never known one of those kind of people before, not counting Amber, who hadn't bothered filling me in on that particular aspect of her personality until this summer, which hadn't been so fun for a while. Were the two of them, you know, going to talk about it? Or—jeez—kiss or something? By the time I got dressed I was actually pretty nervous, but when I came downstairs Dad and Jimmy were camped out in the living room to watch Win's game again in slow motion, and as much as I love Win there were other ways to spend an evening, so I took the pickup and headed out.

I was still pretty nervous walking up to Amber's house, but as soon as I caught sight of Amber, she said, "Hey, baby, check out my wingspan," in this deep husky voice.

"Yeah, baby," I said back the exact same way, "you should take a look at my tail action."

Dale looked at us like we were both crazy—which she had every right to do—especially when we both just about collapsed with laughter, and then we had to calm down enough to explain.

Which turned out to be hard because it actually sounded pretty stupid when we tried to put it in words. You see, a couple years ago—wow, maybe five, now that I think about it—I was hanging out at Amber's house one weekend and we rode our bikes over to the town park, which of course has a lake because this is Wisconsin, and after we'd played on the little-kid playground for a while, we ended up on this bench watching the ducks do their waddling-around thing along the shore. Only there was this guy duck who was totally into one of the girl ducks, and he would not leave her alone no matter how many times she walked away. He just kept waddling after her and quacking in that gossipy way ducks have, like eventually she'd change her mind and let him, you know, date her or something.

Anyway, Amber started talking in this goofy deep voice like she was the guy duck. "Hey, baby, why don't you let me snuggle up against those glossy feathers of yours," she said. "Hey there, you duck female, wanna make some eggs together?"

For a while I tried to be the girl duck and talk like I was blowing him off, but it was so much more fun to do the guy-duck voice that I joined in, and we spent hours on that park bench cracking each other up. I'm sure the guy duck thought we were there for him. At one point Amber said, "Hey there, ducky, what's your name? I'm Bob."

"Bob?" I asked in my normal voice. Because it didn't, you know, seem like that appropriate a name to me.

"Yeah, baby. Bob the *duck.*" Which, again, doesn't sound funny when I write it down, but at the time I was dying with laughter at that dumb-guy sound she was making.

So we had to explain this all to Dale, Amber quoting some of her best lines—my favorite was "Hey, baby, wanna fly south with *me?*"—and Dale either got a kick out of it or did a good job pretending she did. Plus she knew, don't ask me how, that a guy duck is actually called a drake, and she came up with "Hey, babe, this drake's for you." Which made us laugh even more. And all of a sudden I realized my nervousness about Dale was long gone.

Just so you know, Dale Wagner is really cool. I mean, I don't know that much about cool people. I don't hang out with the cool kids at school, I'm not even sure who the latest cool kids are except that I'm not one of them, and the only really cool person I know is Brian. Not that I like him for that reason, but he is. And I don't know what Dale was like in high school because she's twenty-two now. But that's not what makes her cool, the fact that she's so much older than we are. She's cool because she's got this voice that cracks, and she has a great belly laugh, and she drives a pickup with a little camper on the bed, the littlest camper you ever saw, kind of a dollhouse for truckers. She uses that camper too, because on weekends when she's not working she drives all over the Midwest, down to St. Louis sometimes, for barbecue competitions.

Did you know people actually *compete* at barbecue? I

didn't, but I learned pretty fast. Like there are teams and you join up with a team — an amateur team, not the pros, which she said like of course *everyone* knows that — once word gets out that you're available as a sub and that you're pretty good, and the competitions run for days, and there are different categories and special woods and sauces that are Carefully Guarded Secrets. That's why Dale works in the meat department at the Super Saver, where she met Amber, because she was so in love with barbecue when she got out of high school that she studied to be a butcher, figuring that it would be a great way to learn about barbecue's most important ingredient.

"Man," she said, "you get a couple contacts at the slaughterhouses and you don't *know* what you'll get, it's so good."

She said this sitting on Amber's back steps, the three of us eating barbecued ribs that she'd been working on all day with this machine that looked like a war tank gone bad. She hooks it to her pickup like a trailer, but at the moment she had it set up behind the house. Amber's mom, Lori, was gone as always because that woman would perish if she wasn't off with a boyfriend every second, so it was pretty relaxing sitting there, wiping barbecue sauce off with paper napkins and finishing each bite with pop from Dale's little fridge.

"Tell her about that pig," Amber said. Amber — I had never seen her like this. She couldn't take her eyes off Dale. She was totally *into* her, and Dale was into Amber too, keeping her shoulder by Amber's as they ate.

Dale laughed. "The pig, huh?" She grinned at me. "You ever been to a pig roast?"

"Oh, yeah, all the time," I answered, glad I had something to contribute to Dale's huge library of food knowledge.

"Yeah, well, this guy I was working for—Larry—he ordered this whole hog one day, and the two of us headed out to this farm to pick it up. Well, we got there and the guy said that the hog was out back, but the only thing behind the barn was a pigpen. With a pig in it. It just lit up, seeing us. Probably thought we had food. Farmer shows up right then and Larry says, 'I asked for a whole hog,' and the farmer says, 'Yep,' and Larry says, 'A whole *dead* hog,' and the farmer says, 'You didn't specify that part.'" She laughed, remembering this. We all laughed.

"So you had to butcher it?" I asked.

"Larry looks at me and I hand him my knife and say, 'I'll cut it into whatever you want, but I'm not killing it.' Well, Larry can't kill a hog. That's a big job, and messy, too."

"So what'd you do?" I asked.

She sighed. "Only thing we could. Filled the feed trough with sauce and started marinating it from the inside out. Want another rib?"

I laughed so hard my belly hurt—from that story and a bunch of others about mistakes she'd made, confusing cayenne pepper with chili pepper because apparently the two of them are different, and all the things that can go wrong at a barbecue competition, like the judges who forgot paper plates so they had to use wood shingles that someone had brought as kindling.

"We've got to get you to Texas," she said to Amber. "Texas barbecue—it's something to see." They grinned at each other.

All of sudden I felt extremely much like a third wheel. "Well, I better be getting home."

"Hey baby, you taking off so soon?" Amber asked in her Bob-the-duck voice.

"Yeah, sweetheart, I got some chicks to check out," I answered.

"Hey, Bob," Dale said, getting right into the voice, "don't you mean *ducklings?*"

"Well, yeah, baby. But I get around, you know." Which made us all chuckle.

"Hey," Dale said in her normal voice, "I forgot to tell you congratulations on your brothers playing today."

We'd been so busy laughing I'd forgotten them for a bit. "Thanks," I said.

"And congratulations on your playing football. That's about the coolest thing ever."

I just shrugged and thanked her, but I sure let those words—her normal-voice words—linger in my mind the whole drive home.

4

BIG TRIP TO THE BIG CITY

SUNDAY MORNING BRIAN SHOWED UP just as we were eating these eggs Benedict things, and Dad made Brian stay and have some, which he did after only being asked once. Brian said he'd had them before but Dad's were better, especially the sauce. Which made Dad's day, I can tell you. And then Brian said his mom wanted him to go to Minneapolis with someone responsible and so of course he picked me, and that made Mom's day just as much.

Dad wasn't going to church, which has been pretty much standard since his hip healed. "The Lord and I have our own personal relationship," he'd say, which was what Grandpa Warren always said too, and Grandpa never set foot in church that I can remember except for Grandma Joyce's funeral, and then for his own too, although he didn't have much say that second time. Today Dad needed to work on the barn door hinges, one of those projects that was going to take either ten minutes or ten days, but either way it wouldn't involve Sunday services.

Curtis, though, was already dressed, his blond hair so neatly combed that I got suspicious and touched it. "You *gelled* your hair?"

He jerked his head away, turning eight shades of red.

"At least someone takes this day seriously," Mom said in that way she has.

"You *bought* hair gel?" He'd never do that. It'd be like asking him to buy something from the ladies' aisle he won't walk down.

"You look good," Brian offered, which only made Curtis blush more, and work double quick clearing the table just to get away, and then we left, Mom calling after us to be safe.

The drive to Minneapolis was so much fun, I can't even tell you. Brian and I talked and talked and talked, about the football games each of us had played Friday night, and Bill's game, which Brian hadn't seen, and Win's game, which he had. Even though I'm sure Brian has heard so much about Win over the years that he just about wants to barf, he still really praised Win's playing.

Then Brian asked, in that comfortable space that happens in conversations sometimes, what I'd done last night.

"Nothing," I shrugged. "Just hung out with some friends." I frowned a bit, thinking about Amber and Dale. "Do you know anyone who's, you know, gay?"

Brian laughed. "What's that question for?"

"Just curious."

"Not really. My dad has a second cousin in Chicago who lives with another guy. We had dinner with them once."

"Wow." That was a pretty astounding thing to think about. "What's he do?"

Brian shrugged. "Works for some insurance company as a claims adjuster."

"That's too bad. I mean, if you're going to go to all that trouble of being gay, you might as well do something interesting."

Brian started laughing so hard I was afraid he'd drive off the road. "'If you're going to go to all that trouble, you might as well do something interesting'? It's not a haircut!"

"I know . . . But on TV, no one gay is ever an insurance adjuster."

"No one's an insurance adjuster, period." Which is true. Which led us into a discussion of how unrealistic TV is, and from there to how bad football is on TV, how you can never see the whole play, and Brian went on about how much better college ball is in person and made me promise to do everything I could to see Bill, and Win too if we could manage it, although with what pot of gold coins I don't know because just getting to Seattle is expensive, let alone finding someone to manage the farm because we sure as heck can't take thirty-two milkers with us to the stadium. Although we'd probably end up on TV ourselves if we did that.

That was such a funny image I had to tell Brian, and we had a great time imagining the cows, who they'd cheer for and all that sort of stuff, just totally goofing, and then all of a sudden there were the signs saying MINNEAPOLIS.

Brian filled me in on the whole purpose of the trip, which I hadn't even wondered about because I was just so happy to be with him. It turns out one of the customers at his dad's dealership had ordered this really fancy custom pickup, and the guy has it not two days before he backs it up with the tailgate down and trashes that poor tailgate completely, and so the tailgate had just come in for Brian to pick up, and get paid to do it to boot, which pretty much amazed me, that you could earn money just for picking stuff up. I offered to drive anywhere his dad ever needed, and Brian laughed and said he'd think about it.

When we got to the supply place, the guy was waiting for us already, not too pleased about coming in on a Sunday. He did a double take when he saw me, which is something I don't get too much because most people I'm around have known me for years. But when I'm with strangers I'm always reminded of how tall I am, and how big I am in comparison to most people. Like my arms and stuff, and shoulders.

"You play ball?" he asked.

"Yeah," I said, surprised he knew about Red Bend football. Brian laughed. "I think he means basketball, you goof."

"Oh. Um, yeah, I do."

"You play football too?" The guy's eyes went wide.

I shrugged.

Brian, though, was totally into it. "She's Bill Schwenk's kid sister. That linebacker for the U of M?" Nudging me when he said this in a way I didn't mind at all.

"Whoa!" the guy said, his face getting a wait-until-I-tell expression. "So what are you doing hanging around with this moron?"

I grinned. I couldn't help it. I mean, it's sort of the other way around.

"She intercepted me two weeks ago. Scored too." Brian nudged me again.

Well, the guy had to hear all about *that,* and took his time loading the tailgate into the back of the Cherokee, and shook my hand like I was some sort of important person, and said he'd follow us in the papers, which was a laugh because I can bet our games don't get covered much in Minneapolis.

I couldn't help busting Brian a bit as we drove off. "I bet that's what you tell your friends. 'She intercepted me and scored too.'"

"Shut up," he said, grinning. "It's cool and you know it. Hey, we don't have to go back yet, you know. You want to do some shopping?"

Meaning: the Mall of America. Which of course is the largest mall in the *whole United States.* It's so big you need days to do the whole thing, plus more money than I'll ever have. But it was still awfully nice to be there with Brian. Loads of high school kids were there shopping, lots of couples, and I felt awfully good walking with this handsome guy and knowing that people thought we were a couple too. I didn't even mind getting eyeballs about my size because I was with Brian. Plus there were real couples, families with kids and old folks and people you don't see in Red Bend, Wisconsin, the whole world wandering around and riding the rides because the Mall of America is so big it has its own indoor amusement park, with a roller coaster that isn't quite as scary as a real roller coaster but at least you can ride it in the middle of a blizzard.

Thinking back, I can't remember ever being that happy, straight happy, like I was that day. I mean, I get excited enough watching sports and doing them, but it wasn't the same. Maybe you can understand the difference.

Anyway, we did a lot of things I don't normally do in malls even beyond roller coasters, like get my ears pierced. Which I guess you wouldn't do every time you go to a mall or you'd end up with nothing but metal hanging off the sides of your head, but it was something I'd never done once. We were walking past one of those little jewelry stores with free ear piercing—meaning that if you buy the earrings they'll shoot them for free into your ears—and Brian said to go for it.

"I don't know," I said, wondering how you could ever pick just one pair of earrings.

"Yeah, it's probably totally painful. Way more painful than playing football." Which was extremely unfair of him because now I'd have to get them just to prove him wrong.

"Shut *up*," I said, laughing. "For your information, I never got them pierced because Bill couldn't get his pierced."

Brian laughed even harder. "What?"

"Bill really wanted to get his ears pierced so he'd look, you know, like an NFL player, and Dad flipped, and after that I figured I'd just lie low about it."

"So you wouldn't hurt Bill's feelings?" Brian grinned.

"Yeah. And my . . . friend Amber did it to herself and they got infected and it seemed like a lot of work."

"Oh, yeah, it's a lot of work. Sit down."

So I sat down, and he and the girl picked out a pair of earrings for me, one of the six different piercing-stud kinds, and then all of sudden bang-bang with her little gun my ears were pierced. And do you know what? They looked okay. I really liked the way they looked, actually, with my hair so short. Brian kept grinning at me, though I couldn't tell if he liked the way I looked or he was just tickled he'd talked me into doing it. Plus he paid for them.

Then — and this was really amazing, but Brian insisted because he said I deserved something for the drive, and also said that he hated calling me on our home phone because of Dad, which I can understand — he bought me a cell phone. A really cheap one that doesn't take pictures or have games or anything, and with the cheapest calling plan because I only call about four people, but he said that at least then we could talk to each other and at the end of three months I could just cancel if I didn't want it anymore.

So that was pretty awesome, and the two of us spent a fair amount of time calling each other and having the goofy conversations you have with your first phone. He bought himself some stuff too, CDs and a T-shirt I helped him pick out, a Minnesota T-shirt in honor of my brother, which was awfully great of him, and Brian made a big scene in the store, telling everyone how I was Bill Schwenk's little sister and I played football too, and how I'd scored on an interception. I would have pretty much died of embarrassment if I hadn't been so pleased.

On the way back home, the sun low in the sky already, we had our bags from the different stores and my instructions on how not to get earlobe infections and a couple ice cream cones, and we just chattered about football and basketball and hockey, which Brian plays, and what we'd seen in the mall, the old lady who got caught pushing her cat in a baby carriage because cats aren't allowed in the mall, although I argued (to Brian, not the security staff) that any cat that can be trained to stay in a carriage should get an exception, and then Brian all of a sudden pulled off into one of those little rest areas, the kind where there's always an eighteen-wheeler parked and a trash can. Although this rest area didn't have an eighteen-wheeler. He came around to my door and asked me to get out, and I did even though I was totally confused, and then right there with both of us standing next to the Cherokee he started kissing me, and oh *boy* . . .

I have to hand it to him that he didn't even bring up that bloody-nose business because it wouldn't have set the mood so well, although even if the Cherokee exploded right behind me, I think I wouldn't have noticed because this was real kissing. Movie kissing. And my whole body was on fire — maybe from the exploding Cherokee, I don't know, although I could feel that solidity right behind me and I needed it too, to push back against Brian.

I don't know how long we stood there, but I was prepared to stay there forever. All those talks Mom had given, us kids dying of embarrassment, about Being Strong and Not Doing Anything Stupid — which I have to say she gave to Bill a lot more than she gave to the rest of us because Bill has always been an enormous fan of Doing Anything Stupid with girls, starting back in grade school when he dated a seventh-grader — well, even though I wasn't thinking this at the time, looking back I can see how easy it is to Do Anything Stupid, and how I'd have been willing to do pretty much whatever Brian recommended.

But at that moment I didn't come close to Doing Anything Stupid, because right when we were moving that way and I had my hands under Brian's shirt, learning that his back felt even more fantastic than I'd imagined, his cell phone rang. He let it ring a couple times but that sort of thing kills the buzz if you know what I mean, especially when it's the theme from *Rocky*, and finally we pulled apart, panting a little, and Brian with a little sigh answered it.

"Hey," he said. "Nothing." But he couldn't help looking at me when he said this, and grinning because he hadn't been doing nothing at all. "Yeah, sure. See you there." He closed the phone. "I've got to go," he said, kissing me again, a more normal kiss this time, not the Cherokee-exploding kind.

"Sure," I said, because to tell you the truth I was pretty overwhelmed by all these feelings that were turning my insides into giant tornadoes, and a little time-out sounded okay by me.

So we got back in the Cherokee and headed home, although every time I looked at him the tornadoes started up all over again, and when he turned into our driveway he stopped for a second right there at the bottom, out of sight of the house, so we could have a last goodbye kiss before he dropped me off like we were just friends.

And I waved goodbye and went inside with my new cell phone and my pierced ears that Mom really liked, and Dad too, because I guess it's okay to be a football player with pierced ears as long as you're a girl, and I called Brian exactly five minutes later on my new cell phone to thank him, and he thanked me for the ride home like I'd given him the best gift of all, until he had to go and I had to help Dad with the barn doors, which were now a ten-day project, Curtis helping as well, though he'd washed the hair gel out I noticed, and life went more or less back to normal except for the tornadoes that hit me whenever I thought about Brian.

5

SKIMMING ALONG

THE NEXT FEW WEEKS of school my feet were barely touching the ground, like I was just skimming along without too much effort at all. Of course stuff happened, like Friday we played Prophetstown and just beat the stuffing out of them, and even *more* people were there, a bunch of them cheering just for me. I didn't score or anything because I mostly played linebacker, but I sacked their QB three times with everyone in Prophetstown knowing it. That was pretty great. And I was keeping up on my schoolwork seeing as everyone from Jeff Peterson down to Curtis kept checking to make sure I wasn't going to fail another class. Plus Curtis kept reading my A&P book over my shoulder and asking me a million questions (well, four, which is a million for him), to the point you could tell he'll pretty much be Mr. Larson's sidekick all through high school.

Curtis, well, he didn't wear hair gel to school, but he was making some interesting fashion choices.

"It's for Sarah," Mom whispered one morning. Then,

realizing she'd spilled the beans, she changed the subject and wouldn't let me talk.

On rides home from football practice, and on the way to school in the mornings, and on weekends too, I kept asking Curtis about this Sarah person, each time Mom giving me the eyeball to be nice. I might as well have been asking Curtis to give himself a brain operation, but I did finally learn that Sarah went to our church (which explained the hair gel) and she was on the chess team and came to all of Curtis's football games except when she had a chess meet, and she got pretty good grades, which is kind of obvious given the chess thing.

When I asked what they talked about, he shrugged and said, "You know. She's teaching me chess." That was good to hear at least, that they'd have something to say instead of sitting there in dead silence, which I could so clearly picture Curtis doing. The Saturday after our Prophetstown game, Mom drove him to Sarah's so they could study together, and it was good that Bill wasn't around because it would have been like Christmas for him, making fun of that, and then when Mom got back she busted me for not working as hard as I could be, so it ended up that Curtis's new girlfriend got me stuck at home all day doing homework. What do you think of that?

Not that there was much else for me to do. Brian had to work for his dad and then had something Saturday night, and

Amber and Dale were gone to some competition. Plus the whole second half of Saturday was taken up watching my two brothers play so well, and Win did a lot of rushing, which always really impresses everyone, that a QB can run and pass. Every time he got tackled Mom covered her eyes. But Washington won a pretty tight game, and Bill and the University of Minnesota won their game too, and Jimmy and Kathy stayed for dinner to celebrate.

There was some rumbling off to the west as Jimmy and Kathy left but we didn't think much of it. Next thing I knew, though, Mom was shaking me awake in the middle of a huge thunderstorm. Dad was outside on the milk house roof because a tree had just crashed down through the milk house. He was working away with a chain saw so we could get a tarp over the hole. The lightning was going so much that I didn't even need a flashlight up there on the roof, which was good because I had to use both hands to rip those tree branches away as fast as Dad cut them up. Curtis was doing the same thing from inside the milk house, dragging branches out the door. On the other hand, the roof probably wasn't the safest spot with all that lightning, plus the wind was blowing so hard it's a miracle I didn't get blown off. Then when we finally got the tree gone, the tarp almost took me sailing away like Dorothy in *her* storm before we got it nailed down. But in the end we sealed the roof more or less and went inside for some hot cocoa Mom made, Smut crawling out of the basement, where she spends every thunderstorm, to be with her people in all this drama.

The next morning, the sky had that pretty blue I-didn't-do-nothing look it always has after storms, and you could see the milk house roof completely trashed, the tarp ripped already. Inside, leaves and water covered the floor. Which would make the milk inspectors just thrilled, you can be sure, and it was a miracle they hadn't shown up already. So we had to get to work at once repairing everything.

Actually, it was kind of fun. It's not like we're master carpenters or anything, but toe-nailing fresh rafters isn't the hardest job in the world, and ripping up the old shingles was a blast. Although I ripped up one section and almost fell off the roof I leapt back so fast, because there were a couple dozen dried-up rats in this pocket in the wall, just about the grossest thing I'd ever seen. Rats are always part of farm life — there's too much grain to keep them away, especially in a barn as old as ours — but no matter how many times I see one scurrying into a hole, they give me the total creeps. So a pile of dead ones that had gotten trapped there who knows how long ago was not the greatest thing for my morning.

Dad and Curtis heard me shrieking and came running, and Dad was some kind of disgusted when he found out I wasn't even hurt. Curtis's eyes got really big, and he dashed inside for a cardboard box and started packing up those rats like they were precious jewels or something.

"That is so totally gross," I pointed out helpfully. In case he didn't realize.

"I like them" was all he said, and he carried them off to join his skull collection, barf.

The great news is that Brian showed up—luckily not until after the rats were good and hid, thank God. I hadn't been expecting him at all, so it was just as much a surprise for me as for Dad and Curtis. Which might have been his whole idea, to surprise us like that, because he sure looked tickled about our expressions. He ended up helping for a bunch of hours, which was pretty great as well, ripping off the rest of the shingles and lugging up plywood so we could seal it up quick.

And, it was awesome working with Brian. We stayed pretty close to each other, which isn't so hard when you're on a roof as small as the milk house's, and then Dad and Curtis went into the milk house to move the plywood from below so we got a few seconds of make-out time—we didn't plan it at all, it just happened like a flash—and then Dad sent us into the toolshed to get more nails and we got another couple seconds, and all that day whenever we had a minute alone we'd just leap at each other and make out like crazy. It's a wonder I didn't put a nail right through my hand, I was so preoccupied with thinking how great it felt to kiss Brian Nelson, and how many minutes it would be before I got to kiss him again.

We got the roof pretty much finished by evening, not that we'd win awards from the roofing council or anything for our work. Dad wanted me to skip school Monday to finish helping him but Mom pointed out that then I wouldn't be able to go to football practice. Plus I'd miss turning in an English paper and my first A&P quiz, on the skeletal system, which I'd spent all Sunday night studying for. I ended up with an A– on my quiz and a B+ on my paper too, which you'd think would make Mom really proud but instead she twisted it around the way she does and asked how come I can't get grades like that all the time.

As it turned out, Dad really did need my help on some plumbing he couldn't do with only two hands. I ended up going in late a few days, enough that squeaky Paul Zorn worked up all his courage and asked if I was okay, and I said yes so as not to have to explain the truth. Also Jeff Peterson got a note from the school and told me off in front of everyone for "screwing around with attendance," as he put it, which wasn't so fun especially because he asked if I had a good reason and I didn't have an answer any better than what I gave Paul Zorn because I'm not such a good explainer under pressure. But we still beat St. Jean High School that Friday night and I played almost the entire game, linebacker and running back, and Brian won his game too.

That's the thing: when I say that I was skimming along, it didn't have anything to do with the milk house or doing so well in school, or even winning all those football games and feeling like I was really part of the team. It really meant just being crazy in love with Brian Nelson.

6

DAD'S BIG FAT TURKEY IDEA

THE MILK HOUSE ROOF didn't get me down too much, but for some reason it got to Dad. It's not like that was the first thing to ever fail around here, but all of a sudden he was obsessed with money. Like when this reporter called to interview me and Dad asked how much they'd pay, and Mom sent me and Curtis outside so they could Talk. I never found out what happened with that reporter, which was okay because there'd been a big story about me in the local paper with an awful picture and everything, me sounding about as smart as a dried-up rat. After that article, I tried to get out of it whenever anyone from the newspapers or the radio called. I mean, Win and Bill were interviewed on the radio once and all Bill did was laugh at everything Win said because Win sounded so serious, and the two of them ended up having huge fight afterward.

But Dad wouldn't let up on the money thing. At dinner a couple days after the thunderstorm, he brought up, like it was the most natural thing in the world, the notion of raising turkeys.

"Instead of cows?" I said. Because I know as much about raising turkeys as I do about raising giraffes, which is zero.

He shrugged. "I dunno. I was doing some research. There's real money there."

"Turkeys like for Thanksgiving?" I asked. "Like the ones you get free at the Super Saver if you buy enough?"

"These are special turkeys. Wild turkeys."

"If you raise them, how can they be wild?" I pointed out. Curtis snorted.

Dad ignored this. "These are old-fashioned turkeys, the kind people used to eat. Heritage birds, they're called. People'll pay four, five times as much for that."

"When they can get them for free?"

"People in Chicago. Rich people."

Which was an argument I couldn't really take on, seeing as I have no idea what rich Chicago people do. "Sure," I said. "Whatever."

"Well, the sort of money I'm talking about isn't whatever. I got a couple guys coming by Saturday to take a look."

Mom never stopped eating through this whole conversation, so I could tell it was just talk. Dad had guys coming by all the time, like that fellow from the farming museum who would have paid good cash for our old machinery if it hadn't been a rusting pile of junk, or that builder who wanted to buy a field from us just to plunk down five houses, though he offered darn near nothing and Dad in the end realized he didn't want to spend the rest of his life looking at five houses and listening to all those families gripe about farming smells.

So I didn't give it another thought, though when Brian came by Saturday morning, the day after we'd trounced Saint Jean, I told him about Dad wanting to raise turkeys. Brian went off about turkeys and cows sharing a pasture, how the birds would have to duck when they walked under the cows' bellies.

"But they're not ducks, they're turkeys," I said, and we both cracked up because sometimes really silly jokes do that.

We had the place to ourselves. Mom was at some elementary school thing, Dad had a big trip to the feed store (looking into turkey feed, I bet), and Curtis was still sacked out in bed. Brian and I goofed around in the kitchen for a while, making ourselves more breakfast and talking about our games and just really enjoying waiting for the toast to pop up. Dad had asked me to clean the toolshed, so we straightened it a little bit and put away one can of nails and then I found our basketball, which meant we had to find the tire pump and blow it up, and then we had to shoot some hoops in the yard.

It really wasn't fair because I am at least five times better than Brian. Even if he played winter ball I'd probably beat him because I am really good at basketball, and any concerns I might have about, you know, getting too much in his face had been pretty much eliminated by playing full-contact football and also by the fact that Brian's face was where I wanted most in the world to be.

But we played anyway, me shooting with my left hand just to make it fair, and I have to admit that being guarded by a guy you really like who keeps bumping into you on purpose is a lot more fun than being guarded by some stuck-up girl who's trying to get you to foul.

Anyway, I was driving in for a lay-up, Brian all over me, when the turkey guys pulled in, and I finished my lay-up just to show off a little before I went over to say hello. They introduced themselves but I immediately forgot their names, although the guy with the camera said they'd come from Chicago, which is a huge drive and made me pretty impressed.

"So, you want to look around?" I asked, wishing Dad were there.

The non-camera guy shrugged and said sure, and the camera guy took lots of pictures including lots of me but I didn't know how to ask him to stop. I just walked them around the yard and barn, telling them what everything was because I didn't know how much turkey guys know about dairy farming.

"And what's your story?" the non-camera guy asked Brian, who was tagging along.

"He's just a friend," I grinned. "He's QB for this nothing school."

"Really?" the guy asked. He seemed a lot more interested in this than in turkey farming, kind of like that guy in Minneapolis when we picked up the tailgate.

So we ended up talking about the Red Bend–Hawley scrimmage and how I'd trained Brian all summer and how we'd painted the inside of the barn—where we happened to be at that moment, so it came out kind of naturally—and the two guys really seemed to enjoy themselves because, let's face it, it's a pretty good story.

Then Brian had to go, and before he left I gave him a little kiss goodbye, which was the first time we'd ever done something like that in front of anyone, but it's not like turkey farmers are going to mind. Then, remembering my manners finally, I offered the guys some coffee, which really surprised Curtis, who was in the kitchen in his briefs. He disappeared pretty darn quick but the guys didn't seem to mind too much. Dad must have just about talked their ears off on the phone because the non-camera guy had lots of questions about Win and Bill, and whether I was playing linebacker to be like my brother, which is a question I'm getting a little tired of, and what I thought about Win's playing (which was amazing, duh) and Minnesota's chances, and Washington's, all the normal football talk that even turkey farmers can manage.

Finally Dad pulled in and the three of us headed out to meet him.

They shook Dad's hand and introduced themselves again.

"They're the turkey guys," I explained, because they weren't saying that part.

The non-camera guy looked at the camera guy. "Turkey guys?"

"Yeah. From the wild turkey farm."

The two guys started to laugh, and the camera guy said, "Oh, that explains a lot," and the non-camera guy looked kind of embarrassed and said that he'd been called a lot of things but never that, and that actually they were from *People* magazine. "We called a couple days ago and it sounded like it'd be okay to come by this morning. That's what the boy said—"

Dad and I hollered out at the exact same time, "Curtis!"

Which Curtis didn't want to hear so much, seeing as those guys had already seen him in his underwear. He came slinking out, dressed at least, and let on that yeah, he'd talked to the non-camera guy but he thought it was a joke and forgot about it right away. Which amused the non-camera guy to no end, seeing as most of the time people are just about dying to get into *People* and our family couldn't even manage to write the message down.

So they ended up staying for lunch and talking a lot to Dad, who made them sandwiches with this smoked turkey that the wild turkey farmer had sent him that was really amazingly good, and shooting the breeze with him and actually asking a lot of questions about turkey farming. Then

Mom showed up and they talked to her. Then the *real* turkey farmers showed up, and the non-camera guy got to talking about doing a story on them while the camera guy made all four of us come outside for a bunch of pictures, Mom trying to suck in her belly. Then the non-camera guy came back and gave us this little talk about how the story might not run depending on what the other stories were that week and how many celebrities were having babies, which *People* readers care about a lot more than girl linebackers from Wisconsin. Which was A-okay with me.

After they left, Mom gave us the same warning all over again about not telling anyone, because a TV crew came once to do a story on Jorgensens' Ice Cream and Randy Jorgensen bragged to everyone in town and they watched the news for a week, and all the TV ended up showing was a little girl with ice cream on her face that could have been anywhere in the world. Randy still gets grief about that, and the very last thing I needed was someone accusing me, again, of playing football just for the attention.

Right then the college football games started so we had to sit down and watch them, and for long stretches I could even forget what just happened. I'd remember whenever they did one of those annoying athlete profiles that don't tell you anything because those things don't even say as much as *People*, but otherwise I'd just root for Bill, who got two good sacks in and a couple seconds of footage of him with his helmet off, showing what a good-looking guy he is even without earrings. And Win started again too.

That night I called Brian, but he was out with some friends so I couldn't tell him about *People,* which was probably for the best since I didn't think the news would make him any happier than it did me. Because I wasn't the only one who said things to those two reporters, and did things in front of them, that I wouldn't be too keen on my friends and neighbors learning about. It's not such a good idea to go around kissing rival linebackers, at least not in high school football. I wouldn't know about the pros.

7

A Whole Herd of Trouble
Coming My Way

Word started getting around school about Amber and Dale. They weren't doing a whole lot to hide it, what with Dale practically living in Amber's driveway because her real apartment was an hour away. Amber's mom, Lori, was too caught up in her job and her latest boyfriend to notice, but not everyone was, and Amber started getting garbage about it. It wasn't as bad as it could have been because Amber has a reputation for being tough, but she was getting called things in the halls and bumped by accident on purpose, and stuff got written on her locker. She didn't complain about it, not once, but she started cutting school a lot. Which totally sucked for me. Kari Jorgensen, who I'd hung around with a bit over the summer, now had a hot new boyfriend herself who took all her time, and I couldn't hang out with the volleyball players seeing as I'd basically abandoned them to play football, and even though I really liked some of the guys on the football team, it wasn't the same.

Then there was that freshman Paul Zorn. He'd stare at me whenever we were at our lockers, and ask me how I was, or tell me how good I'd played. He kind of reminded me of Curtis although he has it a lot worse than Curtis because he's short and kind of soft, and just looks like a target. So I'd chat with him sometimes because I didn't have anyone else to talk to. Or walk with him, even if I ended up late for class, just to protect him a little bit.

Anyway, one day Amber skipped school again, and so I ended up eating alone in the cafeteria, feeling like every single person was watching me eat my sloppy joes, which are hard to eat in the best of circumstances, and then I got sloppy joe sauce on the health class homework I was doing, which made me even more upset, especially because it's this dumb form on why caffeine is so bad for you that we shouldn't even have to fill out considering our health teacher comes to class every day with a three-quart cup of coffee just so *she* can stay awake. Then on the way to class, feeling just peachy, I saw Paul Zorn get body-slammed by a couple sophomores. Just a few yards in front of me. Paul's backpack fell open, and he started crawling around trying to pick stuff up as the two sophomores stood there laughing, and then right as I got there one of them gave him a shove and said, "Faggot."

I have no recollection of thinking, even for a second. Next thing I knew, I had that kid up against the lockers with his feet a good eighteen inches off the floor and his T-shirt balled up under his chin where I was holding him. One-handed too, which means I was extra mad, because this kid had some

meat on him. Donny Donovan, his name was. He'd tried out
for football but hadn't even managed a day of practice. He
had a little barrel chest and mean little eyes. Only his eyes
weren't mean now, they were really wide, and you could
hear him breathing because his head had made such a bang
when it hit the lockers that everyone in the entire hallway
had gone dead quiet.

He looked like he was waiting for me to say something,
and everyone in the entire hallway waited for me to say
something, and for the eight millionth time I couldn't think
of a single thing. I mean, I wanted to say that I hate that
word because of everything it means for people like Amber,
but I knew if I said this I'd bring even more attention to her
and I didn't want to do that. Instead I just stood there glaring
at him until Mr. Slutsky showed up out of nowhere and
made us both come to his office, and Paul Zorn was left to
pick up all his papers.

The meeting was about as much fun as anyone could ever
have short of being run over by a tiller. Mom showed up in
her elementary school principal clothes looking just furious,
hissing that she'd never once had to do this with Win or Bill.
Donny Donovan's parents showed up too, both of them, just
as short and barrel-chested as he was, so packed into their
clothes that it was a wonder the seams didn't pop. They were
like human sausages, with sausage fingers and sausage arms
and tiny piggy eyes. Mom spent the whole time glaring at

me, and the sausage people glared at me too, and Mr. Slutsky gave this long speech that he could probably recite in his sleep about how violence never solves anything and students should find a teacher or him to resolve their conflicts.

Yeah right, I thought.

Then Donny got to explain his side, which was basically that he'd been walking down the hall minding his own business, nothing to do with Paul Zorn, when I attacked him and gave him a huge lump on his head and probably whiplash. On the plus side, no one except his parents seemed to believe him. Then Mr. Slutsky asked me to tell my side, and all I could do was stare at the table, wishing I had a week to come up with an answer.

"Are you going to allow this?" Mr. Sausage Donovan asked. "Football players bullying students?" He said "football players" like it was a disease.

"We do not tolerate bullying in this school," Mr. Slutsky said. "D.J. will be benched following school policy."

"Benched?" I interrupted. "But—"

Mr. Slutsky shot me a look and I shut right up, glad to be sitting out of reach of Mom. He continued: "We do not tolerate bullying in this school, Donald."

"I wasn't bullying!" he whined.

"Your reputation precedes you," said Mr. Slutsky, which sounded pretty tough to me but it went right over the heads of the Sausages. Then he sighed and let us all go.

Out in the corridor Mom came right up to me. "Are you satisfied? Have you learned your lesson?"

"I didn't—it wasn't my fault—"

"Whose fault was it?" she snapped with that Mom logic I hate. "Certainly not Curtis's."

"Curtis? What's he have to do with this?"

Mom looked at me like I was dim. "Sarah? Sarah Zorn?"

"Wait—Paul Zorn is Sarah's brother? Curtis's girlfriend, Sarah?"

"I'll pick you up after practice. You can break this news to your father."

I also got to break the news to Jeff Peterson, who made me tell the whole team even though most of them had already heard. Beaner Halstaad, who's probably my closest friend on the team and who always has something to say, said that Donny Donovan deserved it, but Jeff cut him off with that same old lecture about violence not solving anything, and how we as football-player role models had to control our tempers, and then he made me apologize to the team for letting them down. Which was swell.

Last summer before football started, I'd been nervous about whether the guys on the team would accept me. Well, I hadn't realized how much they had until now, when instead they were all disgusted that a Schwenk had gotten herself benched for our next game, and with our huge Hawley match coming up in two weeks. God, I felt terrible. Plus I couldn't explain to Beaner, not even to Amber, why it had happened, and that made me feel ten times worse.

The only person more upset than me was Paul Zorn. When I got back to my locker finally after getting chewed out by Mom, he was sitting there—cutting class and everything. "I'm so sorry—it's all my fault—I went to tell Mr. Slutsky, I tried—"

"Don't worry about it," I said. The last thing I needed was some freshman making things worse.

"Your brother always talks about you, you're so nice—"

"My brother says I'm nice?"

"Sometimes," Paul managed, which was pretty smooth of him, considering.

"Yeah, well, it's not that big a deal." What was I supposed to do, tell Paul that I didn't even know my brother and his sister were dating? At least him thinking that, and other people too, made me look a little bit better, like I cared about someone besides myself. A couple weeks later a Vikings defender and an Eagles lineman got thrown out of a game for fighting, and everyone said they were fighting because the game was so rough, but I sat there thinking that they could have been fighting about something no one else understood because you just can't ever know what's going on inside someone else's head.

The only good news was that *People* came out without one

single mention of me. I read it in the drugstore like it was a dirty magazine or something, hiding behind the nail polish display, but it was all celebrities having babies just like the non-camera guy had said. Which was such a huge relief, because can you even imagine how much it would suck to have an article about you playing football appear the same week you can't even play because you got busted for defending some freshman from the kind of name your best friend is being called? Although I bet stories like that never get printed in *People* anyway. Plus it was a huge relief not to have to break the truth to Brian about the turkey farmers — that was a conversation I'd been dreading, and now I didn't have to have it, thank God.

So that was the one nice thing I could think about when people would cluck about me getting benched and how it never happened to my brothers, which it wouldn't because Win was absolutely perfect at everything related to football and at being perfect, and Bill could always talk his way out of stuff, ever since he was little.

Friday night I had to go to the high school and suit up so I could sit on the bench for the West Lake game with everyone looking at me. But the game got called for lightning. Which was great for about two seconds until Jeff informed me that I still had to be benched, which meant benched for the next game, which was Hawley.

Just so you know, I was not the only one a tiny bit bummed about this. At least Beaner was nice enough to invite me out to Taco Bell with him and a couple other players to cheer me up some.

Beaner was in a great mood actually, like he always is, and in no time he had us cracking up. He was talking a mile a minute—which is about as fast as he can run—I guess because he was still so pumped from getting ready for the game that didn't happen. He went off on this bit about the four of us forming a band, doing imitations of all of us, especially me, acting out what I'd be like as lead singer, which of course is the very worst job in the world for me. I couldn't imagine being in front of a crowd of people like that, which Beaner of course knew, and he pretended to be me with a microphone barely able to get out one word at all. I guess it could have been mean of him to make fun of me like that, all my bad talking skills, but I was laughing too hard to care. Beaner never even cracked a smile, just faked a big scared gulp, his pretend microphone in front of him. "Um—ah . . . we're, um, here . . . to um, rock . . . you . . ."

All of sudden, I did a double take because walking in the side door of Taco Bell was Brian, shaking the rain off his Hawley jacket and laughing with some other Hawley football players. I gasped, seeing him across the room like that, looking so handsome with his hair all glittery wet and a huge smile on his face.

I tried not to watch him too much because that's not so cool, and also I had a feeling that it wouldn't be so great for Hawley and Red Bend to meet the week before their big game, even in a fast food restaurant. But I could see Brian checking the room out, looking around for anyone he knew. His eyes worked in my direction and then all of sudden he saw me and — you know how a person looks when they see someone they know, how their face lights up? Well, at that moment his face did exactly the opposite. You'd have thought I was the person he knew least in the world. And he right away turned his back and said something to his friends and in five seconds they walked out.

Maybe I'd made an I-don't-know-you face at him too. But I don't think so. And it wasn't like Brian was trying to avoid a Red Bend–Hawley confrontation or anything, because I didn't get the sense he even recognized who I was sitting with. No, he just saw me and he left.

"Hey, rock star, what's up?" Beaner asked.

"Nothing," I said.

"You see those Hawley guys just now? Chickens! They see us and they fly away."

Which led into a long discussion of the upcoming Hawley game, although I didn't join in because I too busy was trying to figure out what had just happened and why it made me feel so bad.

🌀 🌀 🌀 🌀

Saturday morning I got to play plumber with Dad even though he's not the world's best plumber and always ends up losing his temper. Which he did this time too, up on a ladder cursing away with me standing ready with the blowtorch, which you'd think would be fun but actually isn't, not after the first couple times, when Brian ambled in.

"Hey," he said.

"You know anything about plumbing?" Dad snapped at him.

"My dad's got a great plumber. Want me to get his number?"

Dad snorted like the idea of spending money on a *plumber* was the stupidest idea he'd ever heard in his life. He started banging away on the pipe with his big wrench.

Brian grinned. "That's right, Mr. Schwenk, you show that pipe who's boss."

I couldn't help grinning too. Here I was still all churned up about Taco Bell, and now churned up at the thought that some people out there had cash to drop on luxuries like plumbers, and even so Brian could make me smile. Then when he saw that I was grinning, he grinned back so it was all we could do not to laugh out loud.

He stuck around for a couple hours helping out Dad and me, long enough that everything felt kind of back to normal, and he even said how sorry he was that I'd be benched for the Hawley game. Dad grunted that the Hawley folks must be thrilled.

Brian grinned at me. "Oh, they are. Everyone's pretty scared of D.J."

Which cheered Dad up, hearing that.

Plus Brian—I've got to hand it to him for not shying from tough conversations—as soon as Dad went in to finish lunch, he right away apologized for not saying hello last night.

"That's okay," I lied, because even though it wasn't okay that he'd ignored me, it was way *more* than okay that he was acknowledging it now.

"No, it's not. I just—I was real surprised to see you there. It was like this one galaxy I know suddenly colliding with another galaxy I know. Know what I mean?"

"What are you, an astronaut?" I asked so that Brian had to elbow me, and then we stayed stuck together for a while, long enough that Dad had to holler twice to come in for lunch.

Dad had enough food for an army because Jimmy and Kathy were coming over for Bill's game that was about to start, and Jimmy was so glad to see Brian—seeing that he's Brian's coach and all—that Brian stuck around, all of us with big yummy bowls of this beef stew Dad had made, and Jimmy and Dad with beers. Dad probably would have offered Brian a beer too if Jimmy hadn't been there. It was all pretty perfect until Brian's cell phone rang and he said he had to take off.

I walked him out to his Cherokee and asked if everything was okay, not knowing how else to ask about that phone call that had dragged him away. I must have sounded so serious that he checked to see if anyone was looking, then put his arms around me and gave me a kiss. He grinned. "Just remember that when you're sitting on the bench next Friday watching us win."

"You wish." I gave him a shove. "You better get to the gym, get some training in yet."

"I don't need training, just a big old ice pack, because my arm will be on fire." He gave me one of his tornado smiles and drove off grinning.

I grinned back, but then my happiness faded away, like pop bubbles do when you leave the cap off. I sure didn't have any interest in returning to Taco Bell anytime soon, I can tell you that, not if it was going to make Brian's galaxies collide or whatever it was he'd said. To tell you the truth, I felt a little sick. Things had been going so well for a while there with football and Brian, and school even, and now . . . Being benched for stupid Donny Donovan, Brian ignoring me, that scare with *People* that almost got me talked about all over the country, Amber getting so harassed just for having a girlfriend, even the milk house roof collapsing and Dad so freaked about money—none of this was good. Not one bit. It seemed like after that nice quiet spell, a whole herd of trouble was coming my way.

8

BAD NEWS ON ALL FRONTS

FRIDAY AFTERNOON, classes were canceled for a huge pep rally for the big Hawley game, and all the football players had to come out including me, which totally sucked because some of the kids booed. Although it was hard to tell whether they booed because I was a girl or because I got benched or because I shouldn't have been. I noticed that Donny Donovan was booing pretty loudly, and I decided if I ever met him in a dark alley he would end up one sorry little sausage.

The game was a complete disaster. Jeff Peterson made me put on my uniform again, and go out as an example of Why We Shouldn't Fight, even though if people were so concerned about fighting they should never have invented football. Hawley ended up winning by eighteen points, which is an awful lot different than us winning by seven like we did in the scrimmage back in August. Which I had played in, which only about four hundred people reminded me of just in case that little fact had slipped my mind, in case I didn't feel bad enough already. A bunch of Hawley scumbag players spent every moment they weren't playing just rubbing in their victory, which made the experience about that much worse. So the fact that Brian ignored me the whole game didn't bother me all that much.

Dad made Curtis get up for breakfast with us on Saturday morning, which was weird. Usually they let him sleep in. I'd sleep in too, but most of the time I can't. I guess my farmer ancestors have me hard-wired to wake up at the crack of dawn.

"So what'd you think of the game?" Dad asked Curtis, serving up a mess of scrambled eggs with cheese and little chopped peppers.

Curtis shrugged. "It was disappointing."

"What'd you think of that third interception on Kyle?"

My head came up at this. I noticed Mom watching too.

Curtis shoveled in a big forkful of eggs. "Not good," he said around the eggs.

"There were only two interceptions," I couldn't help pointing out.

Curtis stopped chewing. He sat there staring at his plate.

Dad set his fork down. "I ran into Bill Heil after the game." Bill Heil is the middle school football coach. "He told me you missed two practices this week."

Curtis didn't move. It was like he was thinking that if he stayed perfectly still, maybe we'd forget about him and leave. Like birds do sometimes with dogs.

Mom leaned forward. "Curt, honey, what's going on?"

"Nothing," he answered, which seemed like a bit of a stretch to me.

"Where were you during the game?"

"Nowhere. I just—I went over to Sarah's uncle's, okay? He lives right near there."

"Were there any grownups around?" Mom asked, and I nearly choked. Curtis's ears turned bright red so I guess he also figured out what she was saying. Jeez, Curtis? I mean, Mom wouldn't have trusted Bill mailing a letter, but I had a hard time picturing Curtis fooling around. Although I never would have pictured him missing practice, or lying about going to the game either.

"Her—her uncle was in the living room," he whispered.

"And where were you?"

"In the kitchen," he said miserably.

Mom blinked a bit at that one. Me too.

"We were—we were working at the table," he continued.

"On schoolwork?" Mom asked. She sounded suspicious.

Curtis nodded. You'd think he'd been caught selling drugs or something.

Dad and Mom shared one of their looks. This wasn't going the way they'd expected.

"If you need more time for homework, we can do that here," Mom said. "But you can't lie to us like this."

"Or miss practice," Dad added.

Curtis nodded. There was a long silence while Curtis didn't look at any of us, and then I guess he figured his torture was over because he cleared his plate and went back up to his room, and wouldn't even come down to watch the games.

Saturday afternoon I called Brian to see what he was up to, if he wanted to hang out that night or anything, but he didn't pick up and I didn't bother leaving a message. That's one great thing about cell phones. They keep track of who calls so you don't have to talk.

He came by Sunday morning at least and helped a bit with a bigtime barn clean-out we were doing, changing the wood shavings and all. He didn't once rub in how badly Red Bend had lost. "It would have been different if you'd been playing," he said at one point, which was really nice of him — one of those examples of what a great guy he can be.

"I called you yesterday," I said, working right next to him because it was so satisfying being in his body zone, "but I didn't leave a message."

"Well, leave it now," he grinned. "'It's Brian — beep.'"

"Uh, hey, it's me," I started, and Brian immediately cracked up because even faking it I sound pathetic. I'm sure if there was ever a contest for the worst messages in America, I'd make the semifinals at least. "I was, you know, just wondering, you know, what you're up to."

"You have to press the off button," Brian pointed out. Which I faked, which made us grin. "Okay, *now* I got your message. I was just hanging out."

"Doing what?"

"A bunch of us guys went to the movies. It was dumb, though. We left halfway through."

"Oh," I said, and there was this little awkward pause and then Dad talked about barn cleaning until Brian had to go home to watch the Packers game. I didn't walk him out, though, because I was trying to figure all this out. I mean, I'm not saying Brian should abandon his friends once the two of us, you know, started kissing. And I sure appreciated the time he spent with me, pretty much every Saturday day, and Sundays sometimes, waking up really early just to drive over to Schwenk Farm. That's a lot. But that's the thing: wouldn't two people who spent so much time talking and playing with blowtorches and eating Dad's food, and making out — wouldn't you think that once in a while they'd want to go to the movies together, something like that? Instead of Brian going with his bozo Hawley friends?

Sunday night I was supposed to be doing homework, especially this Spanish paper about what I would visit in Madrid, which I'm sure I'll never go to so why bother. But all I could do was think about Brian, going around and around in my head how much it bummed me out that he'd been with his friends instead of me. Then I'd get mad at myself for being a total selfish whiner like some of Bill's girlfriends who insisted they spend every possible second just the two of them together. God knows I don't want to be that kind of girl, not ever. But I couldn't understand why, just once, we couldn't take a break from farm work and do something fun. Only maybe *I* should ask *him*, right? This isn't the Dark Ages — a girl can ask a boy out without it being a federal crime. Not that I had one clue how to do this. Brian was much more that kind of person, the kind who can ask someone out without needing CPR. So why didn't he ask me? And then I'd start right back at the beginning and cycle through all these thoughts again.

Finally I decided that if I wasn't getting anything done I might as well take a real break, and I headed downstairs for a pop. I must have come down pretty quietly, or maybe they weren't listening, because just as I got to the bottom step I heard Mom sigh, and there was something about the way she did it that made me freeze for a second, even though it was totally none of my business, to hear what she was sighing about. And this is what she said:

"We can't keep this place running on my paycheck."

Dad made this noise of rubbing his chin, all the stubble there, and said in a really tired voice, "Maybe milk prices will come back."

"The government doesn't care about farms this size." It wasn't nasty, the way Mom said it, just sad.

"I'm not selling to a developer," Dad said.

"We've got two more kids to put through college. We've got health care, retirement — my pension won't cover that."

"You think we should sell?" Dad asked, and the heartbreak in his voice — it was four generations of farmers he was speaking for when he said those words.

"I don't know. But these numbers don't add up. What are we going to do?"

"Let me make some coffee," Dad said in the same tired voice, pushing back his chair.

I used that scraping sound to head back upstairs. I felt . . . I felt like that time Mom explained where babies come from. For years I knew where babies come from because of course I live on a farm, and every couple weeks the vet comes and puts on a long rubber glove that goes all the way to his armpit, and sticks his arm in a cow's rear, a cow who's ready to be bred, and puts a baby seed inside her — that's what Dad called it when I asked, baby seed. Because of course bringing a bull in whenever you want to get a cow pregnant is really expensive and time-consuming, not to mention getting the both of them, you know, in the mood. So the vet almost always does it instead, which I guess isn't so romantic for the cow, but I wasn't giving that too much thought when I was nine. And so of course it made perfect sense to me that whenever Mom wanted a baby that the vet would come and put a baby seed inside her as well. Only when I explained this at dinner one night Dad started laughing so hard he had to leave the table, and Mom almost had a hernia trying not to laugh as well, and Bill, who I think was born knowing where babies really come from, made all sorts of fun of me even though Win smacked him, and for years after that whenever the vet came by, Dad would shout for Mom that Doc Hansen was here, their own little joke at my expense. Anyway, after that dinner back when I was nine Mom explained to me where babies really came from, human babies, and that process was *so* much more disturbing than what the vet does, plus combined with all my humiliation at making such a fool of myself in front of everyone, that for years after I couldn't even think about it without feeling sick.

That's the same way I felt now, which makes a little sense when you think about it because both times I was being let in on something that was ten times worse than what I'd thought. No wonder the farm was getting smaller all the time and we were selling heifers we could be keeping to milk, and not buying any new machinery, and never going to Win and Bill's games, and repairing the milk house with blowtorches and duct tape. It's not that the farm wasn't making money — it was *losing* it. And if Mom didn't work full-time — up to now I'd always thought it was sort of a side job for her, something she did for fun even though she has a ton of things to do at home — well, we'd be more than broke. We'd be gone, and all our beautiful cropland would be turned into houses just like had almost happened already, and all our wonderful cows would go who knows where and probably end up as fast food hamburgers.

All my life Dad had said Win would inherit the farm one day. That's what their huge fight had been about last Christmas, when Win had made a crack about how Dad couldn't break even. Did Win know about the farm losing money? Did Bill? Because Bill had backed Win up in the middle of that fight, which is why neither of them talked to us for months. While little old responsible D.J. stuck around— which I had to do anyway seeing as I didn't have a big athletic scholarship to escape with—and kept on working, wondering why Dad never fixed anything or spent any money, and why Mom's Caravan was ten years old and Dad's pickup way older. It was just like the babies thing, my two older brothers in on a family secret while the dumb little sister was kept in the dark.

I'd never thought, not once, that maybe Dad's not spending money wasn't voluntary. That it was the only choice he had. And I have to tell you, as tough as farming is, the idea of farming when you're losing money year after year . . . that's not life even, that's like death. That's eternal damnation.

9

SEPARATIONS ARE VERY STRESSFUL

SCHOOL ON MONDAY was pretty tough. It's hard to think about stuff like algebra when every number reminds you that your farm is about to fail and you'll lose your home and everything you've worked for your whole life. So I was a little tiny bit distracted. But I finished that Spanish paper at least, knowing the grade wouldn't be anything to brag to Mom about, and we started the nervous system in A&P, which meant we'd be getting to muscles next, hurrah, and Amber was back. Though in last period she got called into Mr. Slutsky's office about her attendance with Lori as well, which must have been sheer joy, Amber I'm sure not breathing a word about why school happened to suck for her so much. She came by my locker afterward, and she did a great imitation of Mr. Slutsky combing over his bald spot when he talked.

"Yeah, baby, I'm looking good now," she said in her Bob voice.

"You mean Mr. Slutsky runs around after lady ducks?" I asked, trying so hard not to crack up.

"Duh. He's like the mallard king of Red Bend."

"You'd think he'd get one of those hairpiece things made of feathers," I said.

Amber nodded like this was brilliant. "Made of down. Plus it'd keep his brain warm."

Oh, I loved that image of Mr. Slutsky walking around with a head full of white duck down. We couldn't stop joking about it, whether he'd have it different colors and all. I suggested eagle feathers as well, like an Indian, and that made us laugh even more. It's a good thing Paul wasn't there because he probably would have died, hearing us make fun of the principal like that.

So I started practice in a pretty good mood, all things considered. Not that it should matter one way or the other what my mood was. I mean, right when it happened I was tackling Justin Hunsberger, which normally puts me in a bad mood, even being near him, because he's such a jerk. He'd bum anyone out, even his mother probably, no matter how good he is at football. But it was just a practice tackle so his jerkness shouldn't matter that much. And I'd been in a bad mood all day up until I got to hang out with Amber, so maybe that bad mood cloud was still sticking to me in ways I didn't even realize, and that changed things. Who knows — it might not have been Justin at all, it might just have been the way I landed. I'll never know for sure, though, because life doesn't come with instant replay.

What I do know is that I hit him, pretty hard for practice

but so what, and in that millisecond I landed, I was shot through with pain. Like someone had heated a knife and jammed it in my shoulder. I gave this little wheeze because it was all I could do to breathe, and I put every bit of energy I had into not moving a single molecule because I sure didn't want that pain getting any worse.

Everyone else stood up, getting off the ground in that way you do when you've hit the grass a million times in your life and you know you'll hit it a million more. I wanted to stand up too, stand like you always do. Because if you don't, it means that you're either really wimpy or really hurt, and who would want to be either one of those? But I couldn't.

Beaner came over. "You okay?"

"Yeah," I managed to whisper. "Just give me a minute."

By the time Jeff made it over, I could sit up at least, doing my best not to move my arm. "I'm fine," I said, taking deeper breaths now that the pain wasn't so bad. I hated having all the guys standing around staring at me like I was a dead animal or something.

"Aw, jeez," said Jeff, gnawing away at his mustache. "Shoulder, huh?"

"Yeah." I didn't nod because that might set it off again. "I'll be fine in a sec."

"Mmm . . . You better go see the trainer, have him take a look."

The trainer got my jersey off, and pads, trying his best not to move my arm, and it was pretty amazing how swollen my shoulder was already. He filled up a bag with ice and plopped it on, and right away it started feeling better the way ice always does. Or at least numb.

"Looks like you got a separated shoulder," he said.

"Can I play?" I asked. Because we had Bonnelac coming up Friday, and New Norway the week after that. I was really looking forward to that Norway game — if we beat them we'd be only one game behind Hawley. Which meant we might get another chance to beat them in November.

"Aw, sure. Rest it a week, you'll be fine." He held up this piece of foam, kind of doughnut shaped. "We'll put this under your pad, keep you safe."

It was such an enormous relief hearing that, you can't even imagine. It made the pain go away even more, and my whole body relaxed a little bit.

The trainer went off to make a call, though I didn't pay attention until I heard "Mrs. Schwenk" and I realized he was calling my mother.

"Nothing serious," he said, "but x-rays might be a good idea."

"X-rays?" I interrupted. Because "x-rays" sounds a lot different from "playing in a week."

"Just to be sure," he said to me and Mom at the same time. "Make sure nothing's broken."

◎ ◎ ◎ ◎

I climbed into the Caravan as best I could holding that ice pack against my shoulder, a fresh Red Bend Football T-shirt on so God forbid I wouldn't be seen in just a sports bra. Then we got to spend a whole bunch of time in the clinic waiting room. Mom called Dad to have him pick up Curtis from *his* football practice, trying not to frazzle Dad too much because he's no good around doctors. You even mention needles and he gets dizzy, which explains why it took him so long to have his hip operation.

The x-rays were so cool—I couldn't stop looking at those pictures of my insides. Not that the bones looked like *me* or anything, but it was pretty amazing just how closely my humerus and scapula and clavicle matched the diagrams in our A&P book. It was like my skeleton had taken A&P too, and passed with an A+.

"Well, nothing's broken," Dr. Miller said, peering at the films. Dr. Miller has been our doctor for years. He does a lot of sports stuff, which is good for our family because so do we. "We'll need to order you an ice pack kit to work on that swelling."

"How much does it cost?" I asked.

Mom frowned at me. I'd never discussed money like that before. But she didn't know I'd heard her talking to Dad. So then *she* had to say, "The cost doesn't matter."

"Yeah, it does," I said right back. "Can't we just use regular ice, like from the fridge?"

"D.J. —" Mom started sharply, but Dr. Miller cut her off. I guess he didn't want to listen to us bickering about money. Any more than I did, frankly.

"Let's take a look at you," he said, flipping off the x-ray light.

"When can I play again?" I said, and then "Ow!" because he was moving my arm around, and any time he pushed it across my body, it hurt like heck. Not that he was hurting me on purpose, but you know how it is.

"Mmm. AC separation. Doesn't look too serious, though."

"A what separation?"

"Acromioclavicular. Type I."

"Acro what?" That was way too many syllables for me to absorb all at once.

"Acromio — meaning acromion, the end of your shoulder blade — and clavicular, your collarbone. You've injured the ligament that connects them. But you don't have any shoulder displacement, so it's only sprained, which is good news. That's what Type I means."

I nodded, hoping I'd remember enough of this medical talk for when I had my A&P book in front of me and could really figure out what he was saying.

"Can I play — next week?" I asked, trying not to gasp too much when he moved it.

Dr. Miller didn't answer, just kept working on me like I was an anatomy model or something. Not a person. He frowned a bit, poking at my shoulder. It was all wet by now—the whole right side of my shirt was wet, really, and the football pants I was still wearing, and the melting ice dripped off my elbow onto the examination table, making a soggy lake out of the crinkly white paper. Lake Schwenk. I guess that's one downside to refrigerator ice: you end up in a puddle.

"The trainer said I could play in a week or two," I added, because that sounded about right to me, that time frame.

"Mmm. Keep it in a sling, ice it every four hours . . . ibuprofen, some PT . . . you could." Again, he was talking like he was all alone in the room, like Mom and I weren't even there.

"Great," I said. Only it sounded more like "Great?" because I couldn't figure out why he didn't sound happier.

Dr. Miller sat down so that he was facing me and Mom, so that all three of us were in this conversation. "You have any plans for basketball this year?"

I snorted. Dr. Miller knew all about my basketball—he came to every game. "Yeah."

"It's her junior year," Mom said. "This is recruiting year. For college." Although I don't know why she needed to explain this, because Dr. Miller knew as well as anyone how important scholarships have been to our family.

Dr. Miller uncapped and capped his pen, then put it in his little front pocket. "Football players get AC injuries all the time. Give it a week, add some support . . ." He studied me. "How often do you throw over your head in football?"

"As a linebacker?"

He nodded.

"None. Never . . ."

"How often do you in basketball?"

I started to laugh, but I stopped when I saw that he wasn't laughing. Because that's what basketball is, your arms are over your head the whole game, shooting or blocking or reaching for a pass.

"So what are you saying?" Mom asked.

Dr. Miller reached for his pen but put it right away again, like it was a bad habit he was trying to stop. "You've damaged one of the ligaments holding your shoulder together. It's not going to heal, not very well, playing football."

"What if I rest it *two* weeks?" I asked. I could miss New Norway if I had to.

He looked at me really seriously. Like I was a grownup. "Maybe. But if you go back in and your AC doesn't heal, or it gets injured again, you won't be able to play basketball."

The whole ride home, Mom didn't say a single word. Finally I couldn't stand it anymore. "What do you think?"

She said right away, like she'd been waiting, "You need basketball for college." Which was just wonderful for her to bring up, especially now that I knew our situation money-wise.

"Could I go without a scholarship?" I asked. "If I had grades and everything?"

"Not without us borrowing. There are loans, maybe we could re-mortgage—"

"Never mind," I said, wishing I hadn't opened my mouth.

That night at dinner Mom had me explain to Dad, and Curtis too—who actually seemed kind of interested—about my injury, and what Dr. Miller had said.

"Are you going to get that ice machine?" Curtis asked, one of his left-field questions.

"Yeah," I snorted, "if we sell the pickup for it."

"The pickup's not worth that much," Mom said. (Which was not very nice because it turns out the shoulder-cooling kit only cost about eighty dollars and insurance paid for half.)

Dad frowned down at his fried chicken. We had spinach too, that he'd cooked with bacon so it tasted like I never thought spinach could. And biscuits that were fluffier and more delicious every time he made them. "Did he say playing would definitely make it worse?"

"It won't make it better," Mom said.

"There's a big difference between those two," said Dad. "A big difference."

"You could tape it," Curtis added. "Not raise your arm at all."

"I could," I said, trying my best to butter those biscuits with my left hand because my right arm was in a sling. Mom took the biscuit away from me and did it herself.

"I've seen guys play with cracked ribs," Dad said. "And not

with fancy painkillers, either. Just go out and play because their team needed them. I never thought I'd say this, but D.J. plays football as good as anyone I know. She's got a team that needs her."

"Basketball needs her," Mom reminded him, handing me the biscuit all buttered up like I was five years old or something.

"We don't know the future. Heck, anything could happen. All I know is hard work—you work and you work, and sometimes it pays off."

Or it doesn't, I thought to myself. But I didn't say it out loud.

After that we didn't say too much, just ate the rest of that dinner without even mentioning how good it tasted, me glad at least that I could eat the chicken with my fingers instead of a knife and fork, and then I cleared the table one-handed and went upstairs with another ice pack to start in on my homework as well as I could with my AC separation, which was not very well at all. So instead I called Brian.

He listened to my whole story, and he agreed right away it was the toughest decision he'd ever heard, and he asked me to go through the reasons I should play football and the reasons I shouldn't. He was absolutely the best person in the world to talk to.

Finally he asked, "What are you going to do?"

"I don't know!" All of a sudden I started crying, which I

never do and I really hate, but right then it felt so good. "What do you think?"

"Jeez. As the Hawley quarterback, the only thing I can do is tell you to quit."

"Really?" This stopped me cold, I was so shocked.

"No! That was a joke. You're an amazing football player. Look what happened when you weren't playing. I don't know anyone who loves it as much as you do. It'd kill you not to play."

"And it'd kill everyone else on the team."

"Probably," he agreed.

"Thank you for saying that." I almost started crying again. "Considering everything."

"Yeah, well, don't tell anyone or I'll be totally screwed." Which made us both laugh. Then we chatted a little bit more, and I got off the phone and took a shower, which was a total laugh because I had to wash my hair one-handed. Then I went to bed. Although sleeping with a separated shoulder isn't much fun either, no matter how much ibuprofen you take.

School on Tuesday was a blast and a half because have you ever tried to write with your arm in a sling? At practice Jeff asked what Dr. Miller had said, and I explained as best I could without mentioning the decision part. I must have looked some kind of miserable in my sling with yet another ice pack, because he asked if it would be hard for me to watch everyone else practicing and I couldn't help but nod, so he told me to go home and get some homework done.

Which I couldn't, seeing as Curtis and Mom and I drive home together after all the practices end, so instead I sat in an empty classroom, which is against school rules but who cares, and tried to do my homework while making another Lake Schwenk on the carpet. Which I also didn't care too much about, frankly. Then on the way home we picked up my new shoulder icer so I could at least stop making puddles.

Wednesday afternoon I couldn't face that homework routine again, so instead I drove over to Amber's. I hadn't seen her since Monday—I guess Mr. Slutsky's lecture impressed her so much that she decided to cut school even more—and she hadn't returned my one phone message. I really wanted to fill her in on all this. And maybe we could joke around a bit like we had on Monday. Like we used to.

I rang her doorbell for five minutes but no one answered, darn it. I was about to leave when the door to Dale's little camper opened and Dale stepped out.

"Hey, there, how are ya? Want to come in?" she asked.

I gulped. I'd never been alone with Dale, just the two of us. But I couldn't think of one single way to get out of it. "Sure, you bet," I said, and in I went.

You drive down the highway and see one of those pickup campers and you think a person could barely fit inside—

that's what I always thought, anyway. But actually it's really nice and cozy. Plus Dale had flower curtains in the windows and a tablecloth, and a little curtain hiding the bed over the cab, all that she'd made with her grandma back in St. Paul, which kind of struck me as odd, Dale the butcher-barbecue girl sewing with her grandma. Although she also told me that the two of them used to go deer hunting until her grandma's arthritis got too bad, so maybe it wasn't so odd after all.

Anyway, Dale got me a pop from the little doll-size fridge, and made herself coffee at the doll-size stove, and said Amber was working a double shift and then asked why I was wearing a sling.

So I told her about the x-rays and Dr. Miller and the Type I AC separation, and even about how we didn't have any money for college or the farm, and how I had to decide between football and basketball. Dale sat across from me the whole time, stirring her coffee, and when I was done she sighed and said, "That blows. What are you gonna do?"

I sighed. "They need me. And I . . . I miss it."

Dale stirred her coffee. "I didn't go to college. There wasn't money, for one thing—you know what that's like. But now I wish I had. There's a lot of jobs out there you need a degree for."

"In barbecue?" I couldn't help but ask.

"You'd be surprised."

"You can go now. People do all the time."

"Yeah. I will, someday. By that time, though, I'll probably have forgotten everything I already learned." She frowned. "Amber's being so dumb cutting school."

"Oh." It hadn't occurred to me that the two of them might, you know, disagree. In fact, I'd kind of figured it was Dale's idea. "Did you tell her?"

Dale laughed. "You've known her a lot longer than I have." Meaning Amber's not so big on advice, which I knew well enough. "So, are you going to play?"

"Yeah. I mean, he didn't guarantee that I'd be too hurt for b-ball, he just warned me."

She played with her spoon for a bit. "Amber says you're even better at hoops than football."

I shrugged. "I'm okay."

"Which means you rock." She smiled. "Going to college is important. It's your whole future. And it's expensive, so if you can do it for free . . ." She sighed. "It's none of my business, I know. But you know, I've never heard of a girl getting a scholarship for football."

I was halfway home before I realized that Mom and Curtis were still at school and I had to turn around. Mom was pretty angry, especially because she'd been trying me on my cell phone but it was dead, which I didn't know and which I was learning was a really annoying thing about cell phones. So we didn't say too much, Mom steaming and Curtis lost in his own thoughts, and me so busy thinking about what Dale had said that I barely noticed either one of them, which explains why I forgot them in the first place.

I didn't say too much at dinner either. Sitting in our dingy old kitchen kind of drove home everything I was thinking. I didn't want to spend the rest of my life in Red Bend—I didn't want to spend five minutes in Red Bend sometimes, everyone knowing my business and acting like it was theirs. And I sure enough didn't want to sit at this table knowing the farm was losing money, Mom and Dad not talking about it, and Curtis pretty much not talking at all. I loved football as much as I love anything, and I mattered to my team, I mattered a lot. But it wasn't going to get me out of Red Bend. The only way I could see out of here, away from this busted farm and screwed-up family, was basketball.

"I'm going to drop football," I said.

Dad set his fork down, but before he could open his mouth, Mom asked, "Is that your decision?"

I nodded. It was easier looking at her than Dad.

"You've thought it through? Anyone pressure you one way or the other?"

"Yeah. No."

"I'm proud of you, honey."

Which kind of silenced Dad, seeing as Mom usually doesn't jump in like that. And Curtis of course didn't say a word.

⟳ ⟳ ⟳ ⟳

I called Brian but he didn't pick up and I didn't leave a message. How do you say you've decided not to play football because your family doesn't have enough money for college and you sure don't want to be stuck in Red Bend for the rest of your life with people talking about you every second? That sort of thing you need to say in person.

At least without football practice I'd have time to get my homework done. Which if you're ever looking for something to cheer yourself up is about the very last thing on the list. It shouldn't even be on the list. It should be on a list of World's All-Time Downers, because that's sure how it felt to me.

10

NOTIONS THAT MAKE TURKEYS
LOOK JUST BRILLIANT

THURSDAY AT SCHOOL I didn't have the stomach to talk about
my decision. I mean, my arm was in a sling and everything
so it wasn't like my missing the Bonnelac game was too con-
troversial. Although Beaner did ask if I could tape it or something, and he looked really disappointed when I said no. "We
need you out there," he said, making me feel even worse.
Maybe I didn't have to quit forever. Maybe I'd go back to Dr.
Miller in a couple weeks and he'd say it was a miracle and I
could play now. Maybe that was the solution . . . That
thought got me through Thursday afternoon and all of
Friday, all the way up to the football game I wouldn't be able
to play in.

When I got to the boys' locker room, though (all the guys
already suited up because heaven forbid I should see a guy's
butt or something when I only have three brothers), and they
were getting themselves all pumped and Beaner was doing
his wolf howl, Jeff asked if he could speak to me a minute.
Which was weird because he was supposed to be giving a

pep talk and everything, explaining the last-minute strategy. But I followed him into his little office, cradling the sling with my good arm, and he sat down on the edge of his desk and started chewing on his mustache.

"You know, I ran into your mom today. She happened to mention you're quitting the team." He spat out some mustache hairs.

"I was just—I'm hoping maybe it'll heal and I won't have to," I offered. Because clearly Jeff was thinking I should have taken a moment to share this little piece of information with him.

"From what your mom said, that doesn't sound so likely."

"It might."

"You think it's fair to your teammates, letting them think you're coming back?"

I shook my head.

"We need you, D.J.," he said.

"I *know* that! You think I don't know that? You think you aren't the eighty-fifth person to tell me that?" Which, just so you know, isn't how you're supposed to talk to your coach.

He glared at me as he opened the door. "Bill wouldn't have quit."

"Yeah," I shot back, "and look where it got him!" Which came out totally wrong because I was trying to say that Bill plays college football and I can't, but Jeff just stomped out. And I had to spend the night on the sidelines—and it was cold too, this was mid-October—pretending like it wasn't breaking my heart to watch a game I couldn't join.

At least we won. Bonnelac isn't such a great football school, but still, we creamed them, and Beaner ran four touchdowns so by the last one he was almost flying, he was so pumped, and it felt pretty great to be there with him whooping up a storm and slapping hands—slapping my one hand, my good one.

After the game, though, all that changed, because we all went back to the locker room where Jeff wraps things up, and after he told everyone how well they played and congratulated Beaner, he said I had a little announcement to make. Which I hadn't been expecting at all, but I think he was still pretty furious, for reasons I can understand and other reasons that seem pretty darn selfish now that I look back on it, and I had to stand up and make my speech.

Which was "I'm real sorry but it looks like my shoulder needs time to heal and I won't be able to play football anymore."

"The whole season?" asked Beaner.

I nodded. "Not—not if I want to play basketball."

Which went over like a lead balloon. "Basketball?" Beaner said like he was saying "baton twirling" or something. And he *plays* basketball.

He turned away, more disgusted than I'd ever seen him. The other guys wouldn't look at me either. Jeff told me to clean my stuff out of the girls' locker room, and by the time I got back from doing that, which I didn't do too quickly you can be sure, they were gone.

As soon as I got outside, I could tell word had spread that D.J. Schwenk had quit football. Which wasn't fair at all because when some pro player is hurt, they never say he's quit the team, they say he's on the injured list and out for the season. I could hear words like "quitter" and "loser" as I walked through the crowd looking for Mom and Dad. Oh, it made me mad. And also want to cry because not one person besides Mom and Dale, and Brian too, seemed to understand how hard my decision had been.

At least Dale was around, and Amber. That night I stayed up late with them, drinking beer and eating ribs one-handed because Dale wanted our opinions on these sauces she was working on although how do you tell the difference between three kinds of perfect, and all in all I was mighty glad to be with my two friends. My two only ones, maybe.

Amber even invited me to sleep over, pointing out that I'd had too many beers to be driving one-handed. Frankly, I'd had too many beers to be driving with three hands even, and when I called Mom, she said it'd be great seeing as Curtis was on a sleepover as well—I guess she wanted a mini-vacation with Dad for once, the only kind of vacation the two of them get.

And here's the thing: Dale went and sacked out in her camper, and left me and Amber in Amber's room all by ourselves, me on that beat-up old air mattress I've been sleeping on since my first sleepover there in fifth grade. Dale said that we needed some girl time, which kind of got me scratching my head because isn't that what she and Amber have all day long? But it meant that Amber and I could just hang out like we used to, before she got a girlfriend and I got a sling, and watch TV on that tiny little TV she has and do a little Bob talk and shoot the breeze. We spent a big chunk of time talking about Dale, how great she is — which Amber really liked to hear, that I agreed with her on that — and about my injury and my decision, which Amber completely supported although I think that mostly has to do with the fact she doesn't like me hanging out with all those boys.

Anyway, we slept finally, and in the morning I woke up pretty early as always, and took off because Amber and Dale were driving to St. Paul for some party Dale's friends were having, and I sure didn't want to be the one stuck in Red Bend waving goodbye.

When I got home, Smut just about wagged her tail off seeing me because oh my God I'd been gone *all night* and I guess she panicked like she always does that I might never come back. Which I was really planning on doing someday, but I didn't have the heart to tell her that. It would just make her all worried in her good-dog way. Not that I *could* tell her, just so you know; I'm not one of those folks who actually think

they can talk to animals. But even if I could, I wouldn't want
to bum her out. Or me either, for that matter, thinking about
leaving her behind.

Mom and Dad were still having breakfast, I guess in cele-
bration of the last of their mini-vacation. "Cheese!" Dad was
saying as I walked into the kitchen, sounding so excited that
for a moment I thought he'd lost it. "You'd be amazed. This
guy in Painters Bluff has a factory right on his farm, he sells
it all over the country. You should see his label."

"He's got some more ideas," Mom explained to me in this
tone that made me think maybe their mini-vacation hadn't
been so fun after all.

"Cheese?" I said.

"*Organic* cheese," Dad corrected me. "Organic homemade
cheese. The market's exploding—I just got off the phone
with this guy who's printing money, practically, and winning
all sorts of awards, and selling to a couple big chains—"

"You hate organic," I said. "You always say how stupid
people are to pay for it."

"Not when they're paying him," Mom said, kind of hitting
the nail on the head there.

"It tastes better," Dad said defensively. "Remember that
turkey? Didn't it taste better than normal turkey? Well, so
does this cheese, and it wouldn't take too long to turn the
farm around, get through the red tape so we're officially certified, and we could make it right in the milk house, or join a
co-op for little farms like us—"

"Maybe," I said, "we could raise turkeys *and* make cheese. And get a little bakery going, and a mayonnaise factory, and build the whole sandwich right here." Which Dad actually paid attention to, until Mom started laughing.

"Tell her about the ginseng," she said.

Dad scowled. "Don't laugh—there's lots of money in it. Fellows drive all the way from Chicago to buy it."

"What's ginseng?" I asked.

"A plant," Dad said vaguely. "I even found this Web site on organic vealers—"

"I'm not raising vealers," Mom said.

"Well, half the calves come out boys. You got to do something with them," Dad pointed out. The most reasonable thing he'd said yet, in my opinion.

"But—" Mom started.

"Hell, at least I'm trying!" Dad shouted, and he stomped outside.

There was a little silence, the awkward ringing kind you get after someone stomps out.

"I liked the turkey idea," I offered. "That's kind of brilliant compared to ginseng."

"At least he's trying," Mom said sharply, which only worked to make me feel worse without doing Dad a bit of good. She stomped out after him, only she was wearing her workout clothes, so maybe the stomping was the beginning of her puffy-breath walking thing.

ⓢ ⓢ ⓢ ⓢ

I couldn't believe Dad was talking organic, whatever *that* means. I mean, the turkey did taste better, and I know sure as shooting that our milk tastes better than anything you can buy in a store. I won't even drink the milk at school because it tastes so funny. Probably comes from one of those farms where the cows don't even go outside — they're just kept in the barn to get milked three times a day. A regular milk factory. You mix our yummy Schwenk milk with that factory stuff like the dairy company does and all the Schwenk Farm goodness gets lost. You know, cows aren't the smartest creatures on the planet, but they still need fresh air and sunshine and grass just like the rest of us. Well, we don't need grass but you know what I mean. Plus you have to spend a fortune on grain to feed those factory cows, and on antibiotics too, because it's just as unhealthy for cows to be stuck inside all the time as it is for anyone else. Schwenk Farm doesn't have a fortune to spend on grain, or antibiotics, or fertilizers for the hay and corn we grow — fertilizer beyond what the cows make themselves — or all the herbicides and pesticides and fungicides out there. Actually, now that I thought about it, Dad was right. If organic means not using any chemicals, we're probably closer to getting certified organic than a lot of farms because we've just been too broke to afford most chemicals at all. Which is probably the first time in my entire life that being broke seemed like it could pay off.

On the other hand, what good had not using chemicals done us so far? It's not like people come by our place because Schwenk milk tastes so great, or that we have any way of even telling them how great it tastes. People I know wouldn't pay more for that, not one penny, not for just milk. Maybe city folks would, folks who get fired up about buying wild turkeys that aren't really wild. But it still didn't make sense to me, a bunch of city people who couldn't identify the front end of a cow paying more for milk that came from sunshine and grass instead of chemicals. That's not how people think.

Sure, Dad was trying. But it would end up being another one of his harebrained ideas that never amounted to anything, like that grandfather of his who tried to churn butter with a goat on a treadmill. And the farm would keep losing money, and eventually he'd have to sell to a developer and give up all his cows and farming ways, which would just about destroy him, and me too, I have to say, and that would be end of the Schwenks. All because people don't really care what goes in their mouths as long as it doesn't come out of their wallets. So those were my really cheery thoughts as I cleaned the kitchen all by myself because it seemed Mom was puffy-breathing all the way to Canada.

All of a sudden I caught sight of a blue Cherokee, and Brian came walking in the door and gave me a huge hug, being really tender so as not to hurt my shoulder.

"I heard," he said seriously.

For just a second I thought he was talking about Dad's cheese and that fight we just had. Then I remembered football. "Thanks," I said. "At least we won't have to play each other."

"I'm not the only one in Hawley who's relieved about that," he said, and smiled.

"I bet." It felt so nice having him next to me drinking the last of the coffee as I scrubbed the frying pan with one good hand, moving my other hand a bit out of the sling. At least I could do that now.

"What are you doing tonight?" he asked.

"Nothing. Why?"

"Maybe we could, you know, watch the Washington game at my house."

I spun around to look at him. "You mean I'm actually invited over?"

"Aw, don't say it like that," he laughed.

"You mean now that I quit the team I can actually visit? Jeez, if I'd known that . . ."

"Come on . . . Besides, you didn't *quit*. You'd quit when hell froze over."

Which didn't seem like a possibility now, the freezing part, because just thinking about Brian got the tornado engines going. Although we didn't have a chance to do much because Dad stomped in, grumbling about the tractor and asking if Brian knew anything about repacking bearings. Which, amazingly, he didn't, but Dad dragged him off to help anyway and Brian didn't even look like he minded, and as he walked out the door he gave a smile that sent those tornadoes into overdrive.

Brian hung around for lunch too, Dad grilling him on what he thought of homemade cheese and organic veal. Mom made it back from her walk, all pink and dripping and holding her back, which apparently doesn't like puffing so much. At least she didn't seem mad at me anymore. Sometimes time apart is just the same as an apology. It is in our family, anyway.

After Brian left, I hunkered down over my homework, although it was pretty hard to concentrate, and I don't mean because of the sling. I'd never been inside Brian's house—I'd never even met his parents! Then I started wondering what might happen. I hadn't really been alone with Brian—not counting the barn, which I don't because Dad's there all the time and also the straw is super itchy—since the Mall of America, and while I hadn't Done Anything Stupid, I wasn't sure where exactly I stood on the whole subject. I mean, it's not that I wanted to do anything Really Stupid, but I wouldn't be so against doing something Kind of Stupid— something A Little Silly, maybe. Not that I had any clear ideas, but I couldn't help but wonder. So it was awfully hard to work on algebra, and when I took out my A&P book, I looked through the chapter on reproduction, the pages all grimy from kids before me, and that didn't help much either.

I was so busy with all these extremely overwhelming thoughts that I didn't even hear Mom leave to get Curtis, but I sure heard her return because the Caravan pulled in with a screech of brakes like I'd never heard, and by the time I made it downstairs and Dad raced in, Mom was dragging Curtis into the kitchen like he was four years old or something. She spun him around. "Tell them! Tell them what happened."

Curtis — this probably won't surprise you — didn't say a word. He just glared at the floor.

"He didn't spend the night at Peter's last night. Did you? He spent it at Sarah's." Mom was so mad that spit was practically coming out of her eyes — I know that sounds weird, but trust me.

"Dang, bro," I murmured, grinning in spite of myself.

"Oh, it's funny? That he lied to us, that Sarah lied to her parents — they didn't even know he was in the basement! — that I came by Peter's to pick him up and before Peter can *lie* for him, his mother tells me Curtis wasn't ever there?" She smacked Curtis in the head — really smacked him.

"Curtis?" Dad said in a quiet voice. "You want to explain this?"

"Explain! He doesn't need to explain it." Mom's face was deep red, like that time she got so mad about us not clearing the table. She jabbed her finger at Curtis. "You were supposed to be the easy one! You are not supposed to be pulling this garbage! Sneaking around, lying to us, cutting practice, fooling around with girls — you're in eighth grade!"

"Mom, come on—"

Mom spun on me. "You! You think I don't know about you and Brian? You can't keep your hands off him! You're going to end up pregnant, I just know it."

I couldn't believe Mom was talking like this—about *me!* In front of Curtis!

"I have been taking care of this family for twenty-five years and I am sick of it! You hear me? Sick! One of these days I am going to take my suitcase and my paycheck and I am going to *leave!*" She stomped into the living room and tossed her purse on the coffee table, it sounded like, from the crash of change going everywhere. "Goddammit!" she cursed, which she never does, and then a second later she screamed so loud that the house shook right down to its foundation.

11

MOTHER PROBLEMS

MOM WAS BENT over the coffee table, frozen in the middle of picking up her purse. "Oh, God," she gasped. "Don't touch me." She was panting in pain, not moving one single tiny muscle.

We'd all raced in, of course, and now we stood there trying to figure out what to do, because I at least was thinking she couldn't stay like that, not forever, and Curtis looked so ready to die of guilt that I had to pat him a little. Dad was almost green. Cows, sure, he can stick his arm up a cow's butt to pull out a calf, and wipe them both off with his own T-shirt and not blink an eye, but when it comes to human sickness, especially in his own family, he's no good at all.

"Mom," I said loud and slowly, though she was standing right there, "tell us what you want."

"My back . . . I'm out for the count."

At last I came over and took the purse strap out of her hand, and then with all three of us working and her barking out warnings, we got her down on the floor. Where she lay with her face all white, still trying not to move.

"Guess I better start dinner," said Dad, scooting right out of there. Curtis hunkered in the corner looking miserable, and I guess Mom hadn't forgiven him yet because she barely glanced at him, she just asked me in a non-muscle-moving way for some Motrin. Which was easy enough but I had a heck of a time until I found a bendy straw all covered in dust in the back of the junk drawer, but I rinsed it off figuring this wasn't the time to be picky. And I got her the remote so she could watch TV at least. Then she had to go to the bathroom.

That took about half an hour, getting her up, which meant rolling her on her side, then her going on all fours and standing up really carefully, me trying not to use my right arm because that sure wouldn't help my AC heal, Mom almost crying because it hurt so much. Then we had to do everything in reverse to get her back down as I thought to myself that maybe she should hold back a bit on her beverage consumption.

The whole time I felt sick inside. Not just because of my shoulder and how much I was trying to protect it. Not because Curtis of all people was running around with a girl and he wasn't even in high school. Not because I couldn't help worrying Mom's back was probably going to cost us money when we didn't have two pennies to spare. And not just because Mom was hurt, and in a lot of pain, which was more than enough reason to feel sick in and of itself.

No, the reason I felt sick at heart was because now I couldn't go to Brian's. It was completely out of the question. I'd like to say that I came to this conclusion because I love my mother so much and I knew that no one else in the house could take care of her and help her to the bathroom and stuff if I left. And I mean, I do love my mother, that wasn't it, of course I do. But every time I thought about what she'd just said to me — that I *couldn't keep my hands off him,* that he was going to get me *pregnant*—which just so you know was not part of my big plan at all, thank you very much — I felt like barfing, I was so mortified. And I could not figure out one single way to borrow the Caravan so that I could spend Saturday evening with a boy I can't keep my hands off. Also, how did she even know?

So after I got Mom her special pillow from her bed, and her fuzzy slippers she likes so much, and calmed Smut down because normally folks only lie on the living room floor when they want to wrestle with her, which she couldn't figure out why Mom wasn't doing, I snuck off into the little office and shut the door and, completely miserable, called Brian.

As soon as he answered, though, I could tell there was a problem. "What's wrong?" I asked.

"Nothing," he said, sounding like his house had just burned down.

I'm sure I sounded just as bad. "My mom hurt her back so I can't come over."

"Oh! I mean, that's too bad. Is she okay?"

"Yeah. She will be. What's going on with you?"

"Nothing," he said, sounding better this time. "It's just these guys . . . I thought they were doing something tonight but it got messed up and now they're coming over here. I mean, I really want to see you. But it'd be awkward, you know, with everyone."

"Don't they know I quit?" I asked, although of course I hadn't *quit* football. I had to stop due to a separated shoulder, which is too hard to say.

Brian laughed. "Oh, yeah. But you know how it is . . . Is your mom hurting? Because my dad has these pills — he says they really help."

"Nah. She'd rather just lie on the floor in pain," I said, only half joking. We laughed.

Right then Mom called out that she sure would love an ice pack, and I had to go. Just talking to him, though, even though I couldn't see him, it helped. It really did.

Sunday, Mom was better in that she could get to the bathroom in only twenty-five minutes, and without so much of my lifting her, which was good because she's not the lightest woman in the world. All her friends wanted to help. Cindy Jorgensen even came by with a casserole and told me how sorry Kyle was about me and football, watching me like she was trying to see how hurt I really was. Later I heard Dad on the phone with someone who was trying to get him to make me play, it sounded like. And Dad didn't sound like he was defending me too much either.

Which made me feel just great, that my own father wouldn't even take my side.

Monday at least I got to skip school because Mom decided to see a doctor finally and Dad sure couldn't drive her because just thinking about doctors sets him off. The two of us took the seats out of the Caravan and helped her outside so she could lie on a mattress and make sucking sounds whenever I went over a bump even though I tried my best and finally had to tell her that her sucking sounds weren't making the road any smoother.

Dr. Miller took one look and said she'd slipped a disk and needed to keep doing what she already was, which was lying flat and taking Motrin. And stretching with these special back stretches. And also, he said kind of gently, lose some weight because that wasn't helping.

"But I'm trying!" Mom wailed. "I've lost ten pounds. I walk every day!"

I explained how Mom puffed around the farm, although I tried to make it sound a little better than that. "And she comes back all sweaty," I added. So he'd know how hard she was working.

"Maybe you're walking a little *too* hard," he said. "Are you under any stress?"

Mom and I looked at each other. Neither one of us was going to mention Curtis and how she blew her back out right after screaming at him. Plus there's that money stress that I wasn't going to bring up either. And my injury, which Dr. Miller said was doing pretty well but that I'd better keep resting and doing this boring PT stuff. And Mom's job as well, which I didn't know too much about but I bet being a school principal can add an ounce or two of tension to one's life every once in a while.

"A little," Mom said.

Which meant a big talk on how stress contributes to back pain, which I'm sure just added to her tension that much more. Although at least he said I didn't need my sling anymore. That was one good thing.

Then I had to drive her home, although Dr. Miller gave her these pills that kind of took the edge off things. Maybe they were the same as Brian's dad's. I don't know if they stopped the pain or just got her not to mind it so much, but either one was fine with me.

"Oh, D.J., what would I do without you?" she kept murmuring, which is exactly what I was thinking, but it sounded better coming from her. Now that I was home, I actually missed school. All those kids who'd badmouthed me about football were probably thinking I'd cut school because I'm a quitter, not because I was stuck caring for Mom. Besides, I was also, duh, missing classes, and a ton of homework that

I'm sure the teachers weren't holding back on just because quitter D.J. Schwenk couldn't make it in.

I was getting Mom another pop and me one too, to cheer me up, when my cell phone rang, lying there on the counter plugged into its charger because I forgot to carry it to the doctor's office because I always forget to carry it. Amber's name blinked in the little window.

"Hey there," I answered, relieved it wasn't a kid from school calling to bawl me out.

But it turned out that it was. "Where *were* you!" Amber shouted. "Why didn't you pick up?"

"Whoa . . ." I slid outside, away from Mom's ears. "What's going on?"

Amber took this big shaky breath. "We—we got back last night, you know, and it was really late and she never comes in—" It was hard to make out what she was saying because she was gasping so much, and also because a UPS truck was grinding up our driveway.

"Who never comes in?" I asked, wondering what Mom had ordered. A new back, I hoped.

"Lori! My mother? She just goes to work. But she came in!"

"In where?" I asked. The UPS driver—how come UPS drivers are always nice? Is that part of their job description?—handed me this flat package, the letter kind, and drove off with a wave.

"What, are you stupid? In my room! She caught us!"

"Oh. Wow." I tried to sound concerned—I mean, I should be concerned, it would really concern me if Mom caught me with Brian, these days especially—but the UPS package was addressed to me of all people and I was trying to get it open.

"Yeah! And she totally flipped. She was screaming, and hitting me, and she and Dale got in a huge fight, and she—she kicked me out."

All of a sudden a copy of *People* slipped out. With a Post-it note signed "The Turkey Farmer" and another Post-it note sticking out of the pages.

"We're taking off," Amber said. "Dale's packing the truck right now. I'm leaving this stupid town and my stupid mother and I'm never coming back."

I opened up the magazine and all of a sudden I couldn't breathe.

"D.J.! I want to see you. I want to say goodbye before I leave!"

"Can I—can I call you back?" I didn't even wait for her answer, just hung up the phone and collapsed on our driveway, dropping my head between my knees so I wouldn't throw up.

12

"HE'S JUST A FRIEND"

THE HEADLINE WASN'T SO BAD, really. It was a standard *People* story too, like those articles about a housewife who invents a new thing, or a cat that sails around the world by mistake. The article—well, I've got one here I can copy.

FOR THIS GIRL,
Football Is Part of the Family

"It's just something we do." That's how Darlene Joyce Schwenk, a starter for the Red Bend, Wisconsin, High School football team, explains her part in a family gridiron tradition.

Her oldest brother, Win, a quarterback at the University of Washington, admits D.J.'s playing surprised him: "I wouldn't be comfortable playing against a girl." Next in line is Bill, a sophomore linebacker for the University of Minnesota. "With a gifted athlete like that, it just comes naturally," he says of his sister.

D.J.'s father, George Schwenk, a semi-pro player

himself, coached Pee-Wee football for eight years, and always included D.J. "Not that she would stay away. I knew that whatever team she joined would be better for it, no matter what. I feel that way today."

Longtime dairy farmers, the Schwenks still occupy the home built by D.J.'s great-great-grandfather, although mother Linda explains the house now has plumbing. She, too, takes her daughter's playing in stride. "D.J. was climbing the furniture—oh, from birth, I think. She was always an active kid."

When not playing linebacker, D.J. is a forward on the girls' basketball team, averaging 21 points a game. "In a way, I can't wait for football to end because I love basketball so much," she says with a grin. But when her father needed hip surgery last winter, she left basketball to keep the farm going. "I don't know any other way of living," she explains modestly. "But I don't know many kids who'd want this."

Well, not quite. Brian Nelson plays quarterback for nearby Hawley High School, which has been Red Bend's rival "since the invention of air," in his words. Yet he finds time almost every weekend to visit the Schwenk Farm, and D.J. "I guess it's weird we're together so much, seeing how our teams fight. But she spent the summer training me, and, well, it just seems right to be here."

On the field, though, neither of them pulls any punches. In their first matchup, D.J. intercepted Nelson's pass for a sixty-yard touchdown run. "She's the kind of player who keeps you on your toes, all the time," he says. "I'm not looking forward to playing against her again, I can tell you that."

And afterward? He smiles. "We'll celebrate, no matter who wins. We're good at that."

That wasn't the worst part, either. There were pictures: little ones of Win and Bill in their college uniforms, and one from the local paper of me just after that Hawley touchdown with my helmet off and Beaner jumping on my back. And there was even a little picture on the cover that I didn't recognize because that's not the place I ever expected to find myself, on the cover of *People* above a caption saying "Darlene Schwenk, high school linebacker."

All this was bad, I admit. Those last few paragraphs on Brian, oh boy, I would never hear the end of it. *Ever.* But even that wasn't the worst part. The worst part was—remember when I was showing off for the turkey farmers a bit? Well, this is one reason never to show off. The camera guy must have taken the last picture—or the first one, right there above the headline, taking up half the page—right after they pulled into the driveway. I'm going in for a lay-up, and I'm wearing just my sports bra, which isn't a regular bra but still, and Brian is right behind me trying to swat the ball away, with his other arm around my waist in a way that would get him fouled in a real game but I wasn't minding at all, which you can tell because I have a huge stupid grin on my face, and so does Brian, both of us looking like Brian's arm around my waist was the best thing that ever happened to us.

But even *that* wasn't as bad as the caption—or maybe the caption was equally bad, I'm really not the best person to judge. But the caption might as well have just seared my eyeballs, it hurt so much: "D.J. enjoys a pickup game with Brian Nelson, the quarterback for a rival football team. 'He's just a friend,' she explains."

I sat in the driveway for I don't know how long. All I'd seen was the photo, the pickup game photo, so I figured it couldn't be as bad as I thought. Eventually I convinced myself to read the whole thing just to know.

Then I did, stopping a couple times to put my head between my knees again, like with Bill's crack about being a gifted athlete, which is an old joke in our family that no one else would ever get so why would he make me sound so stuck-up like that? And Mom mentioning that we have indoor plumbing—hello? How incredibly stupid could she sound? And Dad saying he played semi-pro ball—he played in the army, for crying out loud. It was "semi-pro" only if semi-pro means you get out of real army jobs because the captain likes football too. And then when I got to the bit about Brian . . . I've done some pretty brave things in my life, but the amount of courage it's ever taken to drive through three girls for a lay-up, or block a tackle for Kyle, that's *nothing* compared to how strong I had to be just to finish the article.

It was so much worse than anything I could have imagined. Brian and I talked to those guys for hours, we were so nice to them, I even made them coffee, and this was how they repaid us? By making us sound like lovebirds? "We're good at celebrating"—jeez, Mom already assumed we were fooling around. Who knows what she'd think now. What everyone in town would think.

I heard a crunching noise and all of a sudden Dad was looking down at me.

"You okay, sport?" he asked. I hadn't even realized I was lying on my back, staring up at the sky without seeing a thing.

"Yeah," I said. I didn't have the energy to move. Then all of sudden I moved really fast but it was too late because Dad can move pretty fast too, especially for an old guy with a fake hip, and he snatched that *People* up and before I even knew it, opened to my article.

"Give that back!" I shouted, but Dad held me off with one hand while he kept reading, and then I put everything I had into grabbing it but Dad still has some fight in him from all those years of semi-pro army, and I just gave up and went inside because I could not stand watching him read it.

"Where've you been?" Mom called, but I didn't even bother to answer, just raced into the bathroom, Dad behind me already roaring with laughter, and I shut the door and knelt down on the linoleum because I wasn't just feeling sick anymore. I was really puking.

13

A Cabover Camper Really
Can Hold Two People

I LAY THERE FOR SOME TIME, thinking I could just stay in the bathroom forever, with a hole in the door for food, maybe. I didn't need to see anyone.

That linoleum, though, wasn't the best place in the world to be, and not just because it's really beat up and chilly and kind of cramped but also because in a family with three boys, well, there's a bit of an odor issue. Plus I could hear Dad laughing, and Mom making noises like she at least wouldn't laugh, and finally Dad knocked and asked me to come on out.

"Why?" I asked.

"Because your mom can't stand here talking to you."

I slumped out into the living room.

"It's a good article," Mom said from the floor, holding the magazine. "You sound like a good person."

"I sound like — do you know what kind of grief I'm going to get?"

"They're just jealous," Dad chipped in.

"Oh, sure, they all want to 'celebrate' with Brian Nelson. Plus we have *plumbing*—why did you have to say that?"

"It was part of the conversation. It doesn't sound that bad."

"He didn't even mention milk prices," Dad chipped in again. "We talked probably fifteen minutes. You think he'd say something."

We both glared at him.

"What?" he asked.

Right then the phone rang. Mom answered since it was lying right there on her belly, and from the way her face lit up, I knew it had to be Win or Bill.

Sure enough. Mom handed it to me. "Bill wants to talk to you."

You could hear him from across the room. "Hey there, you gifted athlete, when you gonna celebrate with me?"

"Shut up," I said.

"Aaron bought three copies. He wants to know what you're doing with that skinny white boy when you could have a real man."

"Why didn't you tell me you talked to that reporter!"

"Aw, I talk to guys all the time. It was no big deal—"

I handed the phone back to Mom. If Bill had the magazine, if his roommate Aaron had three copies, that meant it was everywhere. I was dead.

My cell phone started ringing: Amber.

Oh jeez, I'd totally forgotten to call her back. And she was leaving town. There's no way she'd seen *People,* not yet, because she'd have mentioned it no matter how bad that fight with her mom was.

I had to get out of there. Off that stupid farm. I grabbed the Caravan keys, and the *People* right out of Mom's hands, and I guess she was too surprised, or smart, to stop me. I flipped the phone on. "Where are you?" I asked, already out the door.

When I pulled into McDonald's, I could see Amber and Dale sitting inside. They waved to me, but there was no way I was going into that building. Not unless it was guaranteed empty of people, which of course a McDonald's isn't—that's the whole point. Instead I just pointed to Dale's pickup and stood by the cab, my back to all those windows, and waited for them to come out.

Amber gave me a big hug. "Hey, I'll see you soon . . ." she said, misunderstanding.

I just shook my head and handed her *People.* If there was one person in the world I could talk to about this, it'd be Amber. That is, if she didn't blow me off.

"Hey, no sling," Dale said, giving me a thumbs-up. She got me settled in the cab and handed me food and stuff, a vanilla milk shake, which is my favorite, and generally just acted calm and nice while Amber read the article. Every once in a while Ambler's lips would move but she didn't say a word, just kept an *f* sound going like a hiss.

"Is this true?" Amber asked finally, handing it to Dale, and all I could do was nod. I had to shut my eyes because I couldn't bear looking at her.

"That's quite a picture," said Dale.

"When did this happen?" Amber asked.

"A while ago. These guys came by, I thought they were farmers—"

"Turkey farmers," said Dale. She handed me the Post-it. "Nice note."

Which I hadn't even read. It was a nice note—I mean, the guy was trying. He said that he hoped I enjoyed the article, and his editors agreed that Brian was the most interesting part of the story. And that I could get copies of the pictures if I wanted.

Like that would ever happen.

"Why didn't you *tell* me?" Amber asked.

"He said it might not even run, and then it didn't—"

"Tell me about Brian! I mean, is this true? Were you seeing him all summer?"

"I don't know! We're friends, we're just—"

"Yeah, 'friends.'" Amber sniffed. "It's gross."

"Aw, come on," Dale said, studying the pickup photo. "He's pretty cute for a guy."

"He's from *Hawley*," Amber said.

"Worse things have happened. So what are you two crazy cats doing, anyway?" Dale grinned at me, and I blushed deep red. But at least I didn't throw up. It felt kind of good, actually. Like we were just girls talking about our boyfriends. Well, with a couple differences.

"He is kind of cute," Amber admitted.

"So are you . . . ?" Dale pressed me.

I laughed—I actually laughed. "A, it's none of your business, B, no, and C, what would you know about it, anyway?"

"Ooh, that's cold," Dale said, laughing. "You'd be surprised what I know."

"Yeah," said Amber, treating this like a big opening, big enough for her anyway, to change the subject to *their* news of how the two of them were asleep—really asleep, not anything else—in Amber's bed, which is just a twin even though she's so big, but her room's too small for anything else, and they were sleeping as close together as two people who are in a twin bed and also dating and also not wearing very much could possibly sleep, and Lori came in to check on Amber, which is extremely unusual because she's not so big on the whole mothering thing, and saw them. And flipped.

Which was bad enough, but the problem was that even though Amber was used to Lori flipping out, Dale wasn't, and she took offense at some of the things Lori was saying, and came right back with how it was pretty disgusting that Lori would go out with just about any guy including the assistant bank manager until his wife found out and walked him up to Lori's front door at eleven o'clock at night and made him break up with her, which says something about the kind of guy Lori picks, and maybe if she wasn't so busy chasing every wimp in Red Bend, she'd notice that Amber and Dale were totally in love.

That's when Lori kicked Amber out.

Although the story took a lot longer than that, and involved Amber going back for another round of milk shakes plus a Happy Meal because we all love those things although the toy wasn't very good. Sometimes they are but not this time. It didn't even move or glow in the dark. All their talking even made me forget my problems for a while. Then all of a sudden I caught sight of a big bag of Amber's clothes.

"You guys aren't *really* taking off, are you?"

"I hate this town," Amber said. "And Dale's got a job outside St. Paul."

"Just some catering work," Dale explained.

"And I can work checkout anywhere," Amber added, which I guess she would know.

"Where are you going to live? In *this?*"

"Heck, yeah. The couple I bought it from lived in it for two years, traveled all over the country. They had a YMCA membership — that's where they'd shower."

Which was an image, all right. "What about school?"

Amber shrugged. "Who cares?"

"I care," said Dale. "You're getting that diploma." She sounded a bit like Dad when she said this, to tell you the truth. Like there was no point in even thinking about arguing. Then she went back in for a couple pies.

Amber and I sat there. All I could think was how lucky she was. Sure, her mom had kicked her out, but at least she was going places. Without a huge stupid article about her in a magazine that everyone in the world reads. "There's no point even going to school if you're not there."

"Hey baby, wish you could come with us," she offered in her Bob voice.

I shook my head, too sad to even smile. I'd be some kind of third wheel in that little camper. Besides, I had Mom. "Wish you could stay," I said back, talking normally. "You're my best friend."

"You too." She gave me a big hug. We both got a little teary to tell you the truth. And Dale came back with a pie just for me, and I hugged her as well, and they drove off into the sunset. Really. They were heading west.

I on the other hand headed back home because there wasn't a single other thing to do. I thought about calling Brian, but it was probably too late to warn him. Besides, I wasn't sure how to explain. I chewed on this the whole drive back, and then just as I turned onto the last road to our farm there was a squeal of brakes and gravel shooting everywhere, and Brian pulled up in front of me.

I'd never seen him so upset. I wanted to hug him or something just to calm him down, but he was pacing too much.

"Did you see it—that article? You've seen it, haven't you?" He rubbed his face like he wanted to wipe the whole experience away. "Jesus, D.J. It's illegal, you know, to print that. It's false representation or something. We can sue. We're gonna sue them for a million dollars."

"Brian—"

"What was school like for you today? Because I just finished the worst football practice *ever*. I almost got beat up!"

"Brian, those two guys, those turkey farmer guys—"

He shook me, staring into my eyes. "It *was* them! I knew it. We are going to sue their butts. They never even told us, just walked around pretending—"

"Yeah, they did," I whispered.

Brian let go of me. "No, they didn't."

"After you left. They'd called but Curtis didn't believe them—"

"You knew?" Brian asked, and all that distress in his face melted into anger. "You never told me? You never warned me—"

"I was going to, but then it didn't come out, I didn't think it would—"

"You didn't *think*? About *me*? Do you have any idea—any clue—how screwed I am?"

You might recall I don't think so fast when I'm being yelled at. All I could do was nod.

Brian opened his mouth to say something else—a bunch more things, it looked like. But then I guess he changed his mind. Instead he just shook his head. "Why do you always do this to me?" he asked, his voice cracking almost, he sounded so upset.

Still shaking his head, he walked back to his Cherokee. He climbed in like an old man, like Dad would, and drove off without looking back at me once. I stood there all alone on that dirt road, nothing but trees in the distance, and empty cornfields edged in barbed wire, and the ditch tangled with dead brown weeds.

14

WIN

OH, I WAS UPSET. It hurt as much as when I'd separated my shoulder. I stood there for a long while, my mind too jumbled to process anything but pain, and then the wind started cutting through me and I climbed into the Caravan feeling like an old lady myself, and drove home.

I sure didn't feel like going inside, though. The very last thing in the world I needed was Mom and Dad. Instead, without even really thinking I headed up the hill, Smut racing out to keep me company, the only company I wanted.

We walked for a long while until I ended up by the hay field — the field Brian had helped me hay last summer when we were first working together and hated each other so much. I sat under a tree on the far side from the wind, and Smut lay her head on my knee and watched me, her eyebrows seesawing up and down, she was so worried.

Why do you always do this to me? I knew exactly what he was talking about. Why did I always keep secrets — only they weren't secrets. I never meant to lie to Brian; he's the last person in the world I'd want to lie to. But I didn't tell him things that I should, things that affected his life a lot. I just wimped out like everyone else in my family: oh, that might make me look bad, I might have to apologize, I'll just not say anything and see what happens. That's what happened last summer. I'd spent weeks training so I could try out for the football team, doing this at the same time I was training Brian to QB Hawley. And because I was nervous that I wouldn't make the team, and scared Brian might laugh at me, I never told him. So instead he found out in the worst possible way with all his friends around him, and all my friends making fun of him and bragging about how good I was.

That's why we hadn't spoken to each other for a couple weeks last August, and if it hadn't been for Jimmy Ott, we still wouldn't be speaking, maybe. But Jimmy made Brian come and talk to me, and Brian was brave enough to do it because he's so good at bringing up uncomfortable subjects and somehow making them okay. And I'd promised myself that I'd really work on talking more, talking about uncomfortable things, because I could see from Brian how well things could work out if you did, and from that big fight between Dad and my brothers how bad it could get if you didn't. I'd promised myself to be brave, the way Brian was.

And yet I'd done it again. And it was all completely, totally my fault. No one else in the world to blame, not even the turkey farmers.

Eventually I got chilled through, even with Smut doing her best to warm me up. It was dark now, with stars and everything, and Venus twinkling away, and if there hadn't been a big chunk of moon I might have been in trouble. As it was, I could see just enough to tell where the path was as I headed back to the house.

"There you are!" Mom said from the living room when I walked in. "Brian called."

"Really?" I asked, my heart doing a somersault.

"This afternoon, right after you left. He said he'd come by after practice, but he never did."

"I ran into him on the way," I said, doing my best to keep every bit of emotion out of my voice. Like we'd just, you know, met up the way friends do. I flopped down on the couch.

"Oh. Okay," Mom said, a hundred questions in her voice. Questions she couldn't ask because that's not our family.

I stared up at the ceiling. It was really dingy, with some stains from who knows what. And a dent from when Bill threw a football inside once, back when doing something like that was the worst trouble you could be in. "He saw *People*."

"Oh. So . . . did he like it?"

Why had I never noticed how trashed the ceiling was? It must drive Mom crazy, lying there all day long looking up at that mess. "At least I won't be getting pregnant anytime soon."

"Oh, D.J. . . . I didn't—I'm sorry, honey. I'm real sorry." She patted my ankle—the only part of my body she could reach. "He'll come around."

I shrugged. But inside I couldn't help but whisper that I didn't think so. No reason he should ever come around for a loser like me.

All Monday night the phone rang, people calling to say they'd seen the article. I tried not to listen but I couldn't help it, a bunch of people asking Mom what exactly I was doing with that boy, in a way questioning her just as much as they were me. Which didn't make her too happy. Dad got stuck telling someone what a great kid Brian was, which I bet really surprised that person after all Dad's badmouthing of him in years past when we only knew Brian as Hawley's snotty backup QB, and it didn't make me too happy listening to this and remembering all over again how I'd let him down.

Going past me into the bathroom before bed, Curtis whispered, "Sorry."

I hadn't even thought about Curtis. This must not be so fun for him considering that kids in Red Bend Middle School don't care for Hawley any more than the high school kids do. "Are you getting it at school about *People*?" I asked.

He shrugged. That's one nice thing about being six-two in eighth grade. You don't have to take too much garbage.

It felt nice, talking like this. I hadn't checked in with him too much recently, I was so busy and so preoccupied. And he was too. "How's Sarah?" I asked.

"Okay. She got grounded."

Which took me a few seconds to remember, that business of Curtis sleeping over in her parents' basement. What with Mom's huge injury and *People,* I'd pretty much forgotten.

"Did the two of you have fun at least?" I asked, figuring that if you're going to get your girlfriend grounded and trash your mom's back, you might as well have enjoyed it.

"Oh yeah, it was awesome. We—" And then his face just snapped shut. "Forget it." He didn't say another word, just angled past me and locked the bathroom door behind him.

Tuesday morning I didn't go to school. I just stayed in bed, frankly. No one came up to check on me—Mom of course couldn't, and it wasn't like Dad or Curtis wanted to take me on. And Mom didn't even make them. That's how well our family communicates. Eventually Curtis had to run down the driveway to catch the bus, and then when I heard Dad head out, I went down to breakfast. I mean, I wasn't depressed enough to *starve.*

In the living room, Mom sighed. "You know, I got a call from Lori Schneider this morning."

Oh, I thought, a conversation even more awkward than the one about Brian. How totally amazing.

"She's very worried about Amber," Mom continued, loud enough for me to hear.

"She's got a strange way of showing it."

"Do you know where Amber is?"

"Not in Red Bend, I can tell you that."

"Oh, D.J., this is so terrible." Mom sounded about ready to cry.

I went in and looked at her. "You mean, terrible because she left—and I'm sorry, but Lori is a worse mom than Smut and Smut's been fixed—or terrible because she's in love with a girl?"

"Do you know this"—Mom struggled with how to say it—"this person?"

"Dale? Yeah. She's really great, and Amber couldn't be happier or better taken care of if she was with—" I wanted to say with God himself, but I didn't think that would go over too well. Also, God's a guy. "Anyway, if you're going to feel sorry for someone, feel sorry for me, because now my best friend is gone."

And Mom did look sorry, I have to say. Besides, she's not one of those gay-people-are-evil types. At least she wasn't whenever she talked to us about it. But it's kind of different when it's someone who spent six years having sleepovers with your daughter. At least she couldn't worry that I was, you know, joining Amber's thing. *People* pretty much took care of that.

Wednesday, Mom made me go back to school.

I stayed in the parking lot as long as I could, and didn't make eye contact with anyone, although you can be sure there were whispers and lots of people looking at me, and I got to world history without a total breakdown. No one talked to me in class, not even the teacher. Then in A&P Mr. Larson handed out a pop quiz on the central nervous system, which was great seeing as my own personal central nervous system could barely function. After that wonderful experience, I found a copy of that *People* picture taped to my locker with some extra stuff drawn on it, and words.

I ripped it down but not before a couple people snickered, and right then Paul Zorn came rushing up.

His face fell. "I'm sorry—I've been trying to keep it clean for you—"

"Don't worry about it," I said. How was I going to get through the day without crying?

"Um?" Paul asked bravely. "Could I—I mean, if you don't want to it's okay . . ."

I had my head against my locker. "What?" I asked. "Just say it."

"Could I, um, have your autograph?"

I stared at him, and he looked so scared that I thought he'd wet his pants or something. Then I started laughing, and I messed up his hair the way I used to with Curtis when he was still shorter than me. "No. But thank you for asking."

And that stupid question *did* get me through, that and the fact Mr. Larson let me eat lunch in his room instead of the cafeteria, which would have killed me. If I'd missed Amber before, boy, it was nothing compared to now. Although Mr. Larson asked a bunch of questions about Mom's back in a way I really liked, like we were A&P equals, and he asked me to say hi to Curtis.

Excuse me, but how did Mr. Larson know Curtis? Although he should, because Curtis is so into my A&P book that he could probably have passed that pop quiz.

I wanted so much to apologize to Brian, but I couldn't figure out how to do it. I'm sure the garbage I was getting in Red Bend wasn't nearly as bad as what it must be like for him in Hawley. He had a lot more friends to give him grief, for one thing. And he's, well, he's *Brian*. Mr. Popular Quarterback with great grades and a rich dad and pretty girls drooling after him. It wasn't like anyone in his circle spent much time hanging out with oversize girl dairy farmers; I was the kind of person that folks like that make fun of. I should have warned him. I should have told him at least who those turkey farmers were. How could I be so stupid?

All through health class and algebra, and English even, I thought about calling, but beyond "I'm sorry" I had no clue what to say. Ditto e-mail, or a letter, which I never write except to Grandpa Willy when Mom makes me, which isn't too often seeing as he almost never writes back. Besides, I didn't think Brian wanted to hear "Thank you for the gym socks," which was the only type of letter I knew how to write. And I sure didn't think swinging by Brian's house would win me any favors, especially considering that the last time I tried that, last summer when we weren't talking, Brian had almost taken my head off.

So instead of doing anything I just thought about him nonstop, wondering what sort of miracle would get us talking again and how I could ever make it up to him for doing this.

The rest of the week I packed a lunch so I wouldn't have to go into the cafeteria, and Mom kept saying things would calm down, although I didn't see any sign of that happening ever. Bill called practically every day to say my picture was all over the locker room and the guys wouldn't stop razzing him. When he found out I was getting grief at school, he said that Aaron could drive over and break some heads, which given Aaron's size he could do with just his pinky fingernail.

Win called as well. I happened to answer the phone, but it was kind of awkward because we've never had a lot to say to each other. He left home when I was twelve and he's barely been back since. He asked right away to talk to Dad, and they spent about an hour on Saturday's game, Dad wanting to hear all the strategy and Win as you know would rather talk football than eat, and they were on the phone so long that I finally went out and started milking so the poor cows wouldn't have to stand there with their legs crossed waiting for someone to get the milk out of them with our patched-up old milking equipment in our falling-down barn. It's too bad Dad couldn't figure out a way to combine milking and football because then maybe we'd make some money for once.

But I got through the week in the end, and even got an A on a pop quiz, which helped a little bit, and Amber called sounding as happy as I was unhappy, and Friday night Dad started a big pot of chili for Saturday's games because Jimmy and Kathy Ott were coming over, and we were all going to sit around Mom like she was a campfire and watch Bill play, and then Win.

Minnesota lost, such a tight and exciting game that even Mom popped a beer, which is weird for her, but it wasn't like she was going to fall down or anything. All she'd have to do is pee more with my help. During the ads before Washington's game, Dad filled everyone in on the stuff he'd learned from Win, and it sure was nice to be there with all my family, thinking of something other than my own misery for a while.

Only I couldn't, because not five minutes into the Washington game as Win was in the huddle and the announcers were chatting away like they always do, one of the announcers said, "The quarterback's brother Bill Schwenk plays linebacker for Minnesota."

"And he's got a sister who plays football too," the other announcer said, kind of chuckling.

My heart sank. I didn't play football. Not anymore, and

those words just rubbed it in. And the five people in the country who might not have known about me now did, and the next thing they'd ever find out about me, the only thing probably, was that I'm actually just a quitter.

Then the huddle broke and Washington went up to the line as the announcers kept droning on. "She plays linebacker, and apparently she's dating a quarterback from another high school."

The other guy chuckled. "That's not something you see in football too much, is it?"

"I guess not. I wonder what the two of them talk about?"

"And there's the snap — and the quarterback is sacked. A great play by defense . . ."

But I didn't see it because I had my hands over my face. If ever — *ever* — there had been a chance for me and Brian to get back together somehow, it was gone now. Having your life talked about on national television like it's a joke — I couldn't imagine anything worse. Amber was gone. I couldn't play football — and don't think watching college ball made it any better, it just rubbed in how much I missed the game — and there wasn't even a guarantee I'd be ready for basketball. I might as well quit high school right now and work for Dad, slaving away for eighteen hours a day while we lost even more money and after a century of backbreaking work had to sell to some developer who'd turn our beautiful soil into driveways and basements, and our cows into dinner.

I sat there, all these miserable thoughts flooding my brain, not even listening to the game. I couldn't watch it anymore. I'd go take a walk with Smut, try to get away for just a bit from everything in my miserable, horrible life.

It was only because I heard a little gasp from Mom that I tuned in at all, and that's when I heard the announcer talking with a different voice, a less ha-ha voice than they use when they're blabbing your personal business all over the world:

"It looks like the quarterback still isn't moving."

15

THE CALL

I DON'T KNOW HOW MUCH SPORTS YOU WATCH. Maybe you don't watch so much. But the next time you're watching a game and someone gets hurt, and the announcers blab away while the TV cameras show the cheerleaders, and the fans with painted stomachs, and then they switch to a beer ad and a truck ad and some ad for investing that no one understands, and all the time that injured guy is lying there with medical people all around him — well, just remember that somewhere out there people are watching at home or in a bar, or in a camper even, and they know that person really well, and they're not interested one little tiny speck in the cheerleaders and stomachs and beer because all they care about is the person lying there hurt. And just take a minute to think about how they must be feeling.

We sat there staring at the screen, and just so you know I will never in my life drink that brand of beer, I hated it so much at that moment, and then —

"We're back in the first quarter, and Washington quarterback Win Schwenk is still on the ground, the medical team around him. This appears to be a pretty serious injury. You can see in the replay exactly what happened . . ."

They played it over and over again, from every angle you could think of, with close-ups, and freeze frames showing a tackle's fingers getting caught in Win's face mask, and the little jerk that Win's head made, just a little snap, and him falling sideways with the ball still in his hands, and ending up under a pile of bodies, and it wasn't until all the other players climbed off him and stood up the way players do that you could see Win not moving.

Mom started to cry. Only it wasn't crying like when you cry at a sad movie. It was — it was the sound I imagine an animal making when her babies are dead. Without words or breath or anything until the whole room vibrated, and Kathy Ott dropped to her knees and grabbed Mom's hand like she was trying to save her life, making these sounds you'd make to an infant, and she gave me a look and I got down and held Mom's other hand, Mom almost breaking my fingers with her grip but I couldn't pull away or she wouldn't have anything to hold on to.

The announcers never shut up, but they never said anything we wanted to know, or answered any of our questions as we watched the medical people pick Win up finally, still in his helmet with huge red pillows all around his neck and big straps holding him to a board, and slide him into the ambulance while a bunch of players on the sidelines knelt like they were praying, and the tackle who'd face-masked him had a towel over his head and looked like he was crying. All this time Mom was crying too, making this sound that I hope to God I never have to make as I'm lying on the living room floor watching my child all tied up with pillows get loaded into an ambulance. And Dad was crying too, I noticed finally, his hand over his mouth, and Jimmy, who always knows exactly what to do, sat there looking completely lost.

The phone started ringing. No one moved.

"Curtis, get the phone," Dad said finally.

Curtis got up extra slowly and shuffled over to the phone, wiping his eyes and sniffling, and just when he got there it stopped. But right away it started again.

Curtis finally picked up. "Um, hello?"

We listened through the beer ads and insurance ads and phone ads.

"Yeah . . . No . . . Okay." He hung up.

"Who was it?" Dad asked, kind of sharply.

"Mr. Jorgensen wanted to know if we knew anything. He wants to help."

The phone started ringing again. Curtis stared at it.

"Answer it," Mom said, automatically because she's said it so many times.

"I can't." It's true. How was Curtis of all people supposed to talk, in the most difficult possible situation I could think of?

The answering machine finally got it — another neighbor asking what we knew, how to help. Onscreen the TV was replaying Win's last play, a beautiful eighteen-yard pass. Before he was put in an ambulance like he was broken in fifteen pieces. Before our world stopped.

The phone rang again. We were still — it was like we were all underwater and we couldn't move, or breathe, or look at anything except the TV.

"D.J. . . ." Mom groaned. She let go of my hand.

I got there finally, swimming across the room, past Curtis frozen in place. "Hello?"

"Hello," a man said, very serious. "I'm calling from the University of Washington —"

"I'm his sister." Numb as I was, I thought that would help. "We're watching now."

The man sighed. "Listen, he's in good hands. But . . ." He took another deep breath. "But he's going to need his folks out here."

"Oh. But Mom — my mom — she can't walk . . ."

Mom started to wail again, like a siren starting up.

The man must have heard it, because he said with extra strength, "How about Mr. Schwenk? There's a flight out of Minneapolis this afternoon we can get him on."

"My dad? A flight?" I gulped.

Mom burst into loud sobs.

Jimmy slipped the phone out of my hands. "I better talk to him," he murmured, shutting himself into the office.

"My baby! My baby, my baby, my baby boy . . ." Mom was sobbing so hard she was choking. Dad had his face in his hands.

Kathy Ott knelt on the floor next to Mom, stroking her hair. She looked across the room at me: "D.J., you've got to go. You have to."

All I can say is, thank God for Jimmy and Kathy Ott. I don't know what we would have done without them. Jimmy came back into the living room with a bunch of information, insisting he drive Dad and me to the airport, and Kathy rushed around packing our bags and swearing she'd get the farm work taken care of somehow. Neighbors kept ringing and sure enough Kathy did find a couple farmers who were so pleased to help — just like we would have done if the tables were turned, which she reminded Dad when he started to argue — and those farmers came right over to learn everything they could about milking our cows, although they shouldn't have bothered because it wasn't like Dad could talk.

This whole time Dad was — well, I was going to say paralyzed but I'm never going to say that word again, not without meaning it. But it was like what had happened took his brain away. Kathy got toothbrushes and pajamas and extra shirts packed in two bags, stuff I never would have thought of like deodorant, and got us in Jimmy's Explorer. She was staying with Mom, who was so upset — she was as upset about not being able to go to him as she was about Win being hurt. Like his injury was her fault. She was almost hysterical. In fact I'd say she pretty much fit the bill of what *hysterical* means. Kathy said she'd call the doctor about her. I hoped Kathy would find time to take care of Curtis too. He was so quiet it scared me.

The drive to the airport took days, it felt like. Jimmy's cell phone kept ringing, Kathy calling with instructions or information, like where to pick up the tickets the university was paying for somehow, which was good. Dad kept shaking his head like he was having his own personal conversation, and every once in a while click his plate, the false teeth he got from playing football, which was the worst injury any Schwenk ever got until this day, that and my shoulder, which seemed so stupid and minor now. We even passed that rest stop where Brian and I made out that first time, and it looked so different now, trash blowing around the trash can, and dead leaves doing a sad little swirl whenever a truck passed. It looked seedy and rundown and not like a good make-out spot at all.

Boy, did I miss Brian. I know that makes me sound awful, like all I could think about was kissing. But I didn't miss making out, I just missed *Brian*. Who I knew, no matter how big my *People* mistake had been, would be as nice as he could be. And helpful at the hospital, asking good questions and being so grown-up like he is sometimes, dealing with whatever it was we'd find in Seattle.

What we'd find in Seattle . . . That thought, it was like some terrible bloody cut that you're too scared to even look at—instead you just keep forcing your eyes to look somewhere else. In the same way, I'd been forcing my brain to look away, to *think* away, ever since that moment Win got hurt, because I sure didn't want to think about what was actually wrong with him. Now, though, sitting in Jimmy Ott's back seat in all that silence, I screwed up all my courage and looked at that bloody cut straight on.

And you know what? Just like it usually happens with real bloody cuts, it turned out to be not so bad. Win had hurt his spine, that was for sure. Or at least they thought he'd hurt his spine seeing as they stuffed all that padding around him before loading him in the ambulance. But all that carefulness doesn't mean a thing, really. A couple years ago some kid in a Prophetstown game said he couldn't feel his legs, and they landed a helicopter right on the field to take him to Eau Claire, and he was playing again like two weeks later. Maybe this was just like that, the coaches and trainers being extra careful.

In fact—I'd just learned this in A&P—a bunch of injuries aren't as bad as you think, not with the drugs they have now, the surgery, and physical therapy. People hear "spine injury" and flip out, but often the person just walks with a cane, or their fingers are a little numb or something. Or nothing's wrong, even. Now I was kicking myself that I hadn't thought to bring my notes. But I still remembered a lot, and everything I remembered made me feel a little less worried, a little less tight and sick inside, about Win. Maybe this wouldn't be so awful. Maybe when we showed up, Win would have one of those whiplash collars on and just be bummed he'd missed the game. Maybe that wouldn't happen, but maybe it would.

Then Bill called from Pennsylvania where they'd just played and said he was going to fly out to Seattle tomorrow, on the very first plane he could.

The relief I felt at hearing this — you can't even imagine. Because Bill is Win's closest relative, and a real legal grown-up. He'd have a great time busting Win in his whiplash collar, making fun of Win being so serious. He'd be enthusiastic and positive, not like me or Dad. Dad can't *stand* hospitals; he passes out around needles all the time. And Dad had never even been on a plane, not that I could remember. Mom and us four kids flew to Florida every couple years to visit Mom's father and his second wife, Charmel, who Mom doesn't get along with so well. But Dad stayed in Red Bend and took care of the farm and said it was a heck of a lot easier than being stuck in that little condo with all that family tension. The few times we went on a real family vacation with all six of us, which is pretty much never because that means hiring a farmer to do our milking, we'd drive to Lake Superior or something and then sit in a circle watching Dad worry about his cows. Which wasn't so much fun. There was no way that

Dad—who's so good at milking and cooking, and so good at thinking up harebrained ideas—there was no way he'd be able to handle this, not without me and Bill there beside him.

We finally made it to that enormous Minneapolis airport with just minutes to spare. I'd been here before, those times we went to Florida, but I was still glad Jimmy walked us in because it's pretty confusing.

Dad's hands were shaking, I could see.

"The cows will be okay," I said.

"Curtis isn't you, sport," he said, his voice shaking too. Right as we'd pulled away from the house, he'd told Curtis to watch the farmers, make sure they were doing everything correctly. That's a big responsibility to give to a kid who doesn't talk. "And I—I feel for your mother."

"Kathy's with her," Jimmy chipped in. "She's a real pro at this."

Our words didn't seem to help, though. Dad still looked sick.

This is too much for him. I didn't say anything as we walked, but I couldn't keep that thought out of my brain. And you know, it was the strangest thing, but I didn't think less of him for it. I've been through patches where I really hated Dad, but we've been getting along better recently. Maybe I can just get inside his head a bit more, I don't know. Like his needle thing—that's not his fault, that's just who he is, like being left-handed or something. And thinking Curtis couldn't manage the farm — that was just plain obvious. And wanting to be with Mom . . . Win was going to have doctors all around him, and nurses, the whole University of Washington probably, not to mention me and Bill. Mom didn't have anyone except Kathy Ott. Right now she needed Dad as much as Win did. Maybe more.

Just then Jimmy found the ticket lady we were supposed to meet, the one who was going to hustle us past all those people who didn't have family medical emergencies and weren't late.

"Okay then, I just need to see some ID," she said.

Dad started going through his wallet, his hands shaking worse than ever.

"Wait," I said.

Everyone looked at me.

"Dad . . . Bill and I can do this."

"What?" said Dad, blinking at these words.

"You go back home. They need you there."

"No — my son —" Dad started to cry.

Jimmy Ott put his arm around him in that way men do. In Wisconsin anyway.

"My cousin got in a motorcycle accident," the ticket lady chipped in, "and the first couple days don't matter, really. He won't remember much anyway."

I looked Dad in the eyes. "Win's going to be okay. You

know him. He's going to be fine." I knew this in my bones. I knew it like I'd known it my entire sixteen years of life.

"Maybe I could fly out in a couple days . . ." Dad whispered. "Get things organized first."

Jimmy turned to the ticket lady. "Can we do that?"

The ticket lady started working away at her computer.

"Let me do this, Dad," I said, feeling so strong and capable. "You take care of Mom. Let me and Bill handle this."

"Oh, sport." Dad's voice cracked. "Okay," he whispered.

"I'm proud of you, D.J.," Jimmy said, getting teary-eyed himself.

Dad hugged me so hard that I thought I might snap in two. It felt good, though, that hug. "I'm so proud of you, sport," he whispered.

The lady handed over my tickets. "There you go now. Now just follow me . . ."

"Thanks for all your help," Jimmy said. "By the way, how's your cousin doing there?"

"Oh," she said brightly, like this was the best news she'd ever had, "he's off his ventilator for half an hour at a time now."

That was pretty much all I could think about in the mad rush to the plane. At least the flight attendant lady who took me to my seat didn't mention any relatives of hers who happened to be double amputees and thrilled to bits about it.

A *ventilator?* Why did she have to bring that up? Thank God I wasn't flying with Dad, because that word knocked him out. It was going to be a long ride home for him and Jimmy.

I hoped Dad wouldn't say "ventilator" to Mom anytime soon, because that wasn't Win's injury at all—which I shouted to him as the ticket lady trotted me away, that Win could breathe so he shouldn't worry. I knew this for a fact because I'd seen little puffs of steam coming out of his face mask when the TV showed the medical people taking care of him. Whatever it was that was broken, or what they thought was broken, wasn't so high up his neck that it interfered with his breathing. The highest spine bones, the vertebrae, they have the nerves for breathing, then lower ones control shoulders and arms, then hands and fingers, and right on down your body. Now I wished even more I'd brought my A&P notes, and that I'd paid even more attention in class, but who ever thinks that what they're learning might actually, you know, matter? Not me. I never once thought, sitting there in Mr. Larson's front row, that a week later I'd be flying on a plane all by myself to a real honest-to-God injury.

Actually, now that I had time to think about it—and I had more than enough time to think, seeing as the flight took forever and the plane was completely quiet, which I'd never experienced before traveling with three brothers and a mom shushing us every second—this whole thing was kind of cool. Here I'd been whining for weeks about wanting to get out of Red Bend, get away from that stupid high school, and all of a sudden I was. Not that I wanted Win to be hurt—oh God, no—but not many sixteen-year-olds get to fly across the country by themselves. And then maybe once Bill showed up and the two of us were sure Win was okay and the doctors were doing all the things they could, then I could call Brian and apologize about *People,* and he'd talk to me because that's what a good guy he is, and I could tell him the story of Curtis ignoring the turkey guys' phone call, which might make him laugh even, now that we'd both had a chance to calm down.

We landed, and waiting outside security was a guy who was clearly a football coach, and it wasn't just the Washington jacket—it was the way he stood and everything. He came right up to me and shook my hand, said his name was Charlie Wright and that he recognized me right away, which I guess was one good thing about *People.* He didn't say too much as we walked through the airport, just that it didn't look like Win needed surgery, and how glad he was that I could come out on such short notice and how he understood about Dad. Which I guess he'd learned while I was on the plane.

We drove right to the hospital, which was even bigger and shinier and scary-looking than I had imagined, and I was awfully glad Charlie Wright was with me. He walked in kind of holding my arm, which I really appreciated, and took me up to a floor with nurses everywhere and blinking lights, worried folks standing in little groups outside each patient's room. There was one room so full of people and machinery I could barely see the bed, and Charlie stopped one of the nurses, and she looked at me and said I could go in.

"Complete idiot." That's a pretty graphic description. "Total moron" is another one. There are some curse words too, for a person who is absolutely stupid and worthless. But I can't think of anything strong enough to explain how I felt at that moment, how completely disgusted I was with myself for thinking that maybe Win would be wearing a whiplash collar and chatting it up, or that it was pretty cool for a sixteen-year-old girl to fly here all alone and get away from all those jawing people in Red Bend, or that maybe because of Win's injury I'd be able to hang out with Bill, and maybe even reconnect with Brian.

Because, I now knew, all that thinking was dead wrong. Because now I could see a person lying in the bed with tubes coming out of his mouth and nose and arms, wires hooked up everywhere and a big plastic collar strapped hard around his neck, his closed eyes like bruises, and his skin looking almost green in that hospital light. That was my brother.

16

THE MOST DIFFICULT SITUATION
I CAN THINK OF

WIN'S HANDS WERE DIRTY. Isn't that weird? His fingers still had grass stains on them, and bits of dirt under his nails the way you get when you play football. When *he'd* played football.

I reached out without even really thinking. His fingers were warm even though Win didn't look alive at all. If they'd been stone cold, I wouldn't have been a bit surprised.

"You can touch him," a nurse said, though I already was. I'd forgotten other people were in the room, I was so busy thinking that it wasn't Win in the hospital bed all surrounded by tubes and wires and blinking lights. It was someone else. Not that they'd switched bodies or anything, though I'd have believed that in a heartbeat if there was a chance in heck it were true. But that it was someone else altogether.

"It's not as bad as it looks," the nurse continued, although I sure didn't see how that could be the case. She pointed to that hard plastic cuff around his neck, so tight his chin looked jammed in. "That's called a cervical collar—"

"To keep his neck from moving. Until the bones can knit," I said.

You know how when you touch something hot, your hand jerks back right away? That's because it's a reflex. Because if your brain had to take the time to process it, you might end up pretty burned.

That same thing was happening right now. My reflexes were taking over, if you want to think of it that way, and shutting down all those emotion parts of my brain so I could survive. Not that I wanted this to happen. I wanted to burst into tears and demand they fix Win right away and make him back the way he was. But I couldn't. Until Bill arrived, I was the Responsible One.

Even so, when Charlie Wright put his arm around my shoulders, it was all I could do not to lose it. We stood there for a while, him respecting my silence in a way I really appreciated, and then a nurse said that Win's doctor was available if I wanted to talk.

"Sure," I said reflexively, my brain barely even registering.

Dr. Rosenberger was very tall and thin, with gray hair like doctors always have. He brought me into a little private room made for talks like this, and brought Charlie too, when I said it was okay, and said how difficult this must be and he'd explain as best he could.

"Did you give him the steroids yet?" I asked.

"Steroids!" asked Charlie Wright. "What are you talking about? The NCAA would never allow—"

Dr. Rosenberger blinked, and examined me. "Have you been online?"

"No, I . . . we were just studying this. In school."

The doctor turned to Charlie Wright. "Not 'steroids.' A cortisone drug that reduces swelling in the spinal cord." He faced me again. "We administered it twenty-three minutes after the incident. That's as good as it could possibly be. Do you know what C6 means? C5?"

I nodded. "Cervical vertebrae. Does this mean he can still move his shoulders?"

The doctor frowned a bit. "That's a very good question. We won't know his exact situation until the swelling goes down. But his shoulders, definitely. The rest . . . His spinal cord wasn't severed, only bruised. A C5 or C6 is a world of difference from C2. Your brother's very fortunate."

"If he was fortunate, he wouldn't be here," I said. I guess when the emotion part of my brain turned off, the tact went too.

If Dr. Rosenberger was offended, though, he didn't bat an eye. Instead he went on to tell us a whole bunch more medical stuff, how Win's injury was incomplete because the spinal cord itself wasn't broken, just the bones, and that it was stable because the ligaments weren't damaged. And even though he kept telling me not to get too optimistic, not yet, I couldn't help but notice that *incomplete* and *stable* sounded better than *completely unstable*. Then he explained how the Philadelphia collar — that's the official name for that cervical collar Win had on—would keep his neck from moving until the broken vertebrae reknitted, and for some reason all I could think about was Philadelphia cream cheese and how cream cheese wouldn't keep Win's neck stable at all.

Just then the phone rang. Dr. Rosenberger answered, and looked at me. "It's your parents."

How's that for stupid? I'd turned off my cell phone on the plane when the lady asked me to and I hadn't even thought to turn it back on again.

He handed me the phone. "Tomorrow we'll have a conference call with your folks. Right now work on getting some sleep." He smiled at me. "That was a good article. I really enjoyed it."

He and Charlie left. I sat there blinking, figuring out finally that he was talking about *People.*

"So . . . how's he look?" Mom asked, her voice quavering.

"He—he's okay," I said. What was I supposed to say? That her son looked like a piece of roadkill? That he had more tubes in him than a basement?

"What'd he have to say?"

"He's sleeping, so he didn't talk too much. You know how important sleeping is."

"You better warn him, sport," said Dad. "Those hospital painkillers will bind you up. You gotta be careful."

"Okay." There again, what was I supposed to say—that

constipation probably wasn't the biggest issue in Win's life right now? Sure.

"Oh, George!" Mom said. "Listen, when should we come out? What'd the doctors say?"

"Um . . . let's wait for Bill to get here first." Which led to a long discussion about Bill and his travel plans, which they knew all about because they'd talked to him a bunch already. I kept dodging their Win questions by repeating what Dr. Rosenberger had said, that we wouldn't know anything for a couple days, and filling them in about complete and stable and Philadelphia collars, only without using the words "cream cheese," and trying to sound as with it as I could, which was hard.

I got off the phone at last, totally exhausted, and got hit right away with another problem: where was I going to sleep? I hadn't even thought about it, though I did still have my little duffel with my toothbrush and everything. Maybe I could crash on one of those waiting room couches.

When I wandered out into the hall, though, Charlie Wright was standing there. "Why don't you come home to our place?"

I looked toward Win's room, the nurses working away.

"They'll take care of him tonight," Charlie said. "You need to rest."

So I followed him back outside. Charlie mentioned how impressive I'd sounded, how mature, even though I didn't feel either one of those things, not a speck. All I felt was beat. I'd changed my mind: I should not be here. This was Mom's job, this is what moms do, it comes automatically with having babies. They learn it in the hospital giving birth, probably. Or Bill, or Mr. Larson even, because he knows all about spines. Whoever should be here, it wasn't me.

We didn't say much in the car. Charlie pulled into a nice house on a street of same-looking houses—probably a dairy farm once. We walked in and Marla, his wife, gave me a big hug, and she wouldn't let go, she kept hugging and hugging until I felt this little pop inside me, and all that exhaustion and resentment and maturity collapsed like a dam breaking, and I sobbed onto her shoulder like my organs, not just my heart but my liver and kidneys too, all those organs we haven't covered yet in A&P, were being ripped right out of my body.

Guess how well I slept. Even though Marla has a very nice guest room and promised to keep the kids quiet. But I was awake at five anyway, because of the time change and just because. Charlie drove me back to the hospital. I told him he didn't need to do all this but he said that after four years he considered Win a son and wouldn't be anywhere else in the world.

I went into Win's room. He was awake, it looked like, staring at the ceiling.

"Hey, Win," I said. The nurse nudged me until I was standing almost right over him, which felt weird but it was the only way he could see me with his neck so locked up.

"Hey," he whispered. The tube was out of his mouth at least. That was nice, knowing he really could breathe on his own.

"You look good." That was the best I could come up with — isn't that pathetic?

"No, I don't." He wasn't joking, either.

"Yeah, well . . . this is something, all right. Mom wanted to come so much, but her back—" I felt like such an idiot. Like, oh your neck is broken and everything but Mom is *really* hurt. Plus I couldn't even figure out what to say about Dad.

"Could you do me a favor, D.J.?" Win whispered.

"Sure. Anything."

"Get out of this room and don't come back. And keep everyone out. Including Charlie."

"Oh," I said. I mean, what do you say to that? What can you possibly say? "Um, okay." And I stumbled backwards, feeling my way out of the room because my eyes barely worked. That's how much his words hurt me. Like I'd been punched in the stomach.

Out in the hall, Charlie asked how he was.

"He, well, he doesn't want to see anyone right now."

"Makes sense," Charlie said. He didn't seem fazed at all.

So we settled in a waiting room. Charlie kept telling me

stories about Win. How he had both playbooks memorized on the first day of practice, offense and defense, so he'd know everything that was going on. How he took the underclassmen under his wing and got on their butts and had special morning workouts for them, just like he used to in high school. How he went to Marla Wright's exercise classes because she said this thing called Pilates helps your core strength and even though he was the only guy in the room, and about four times bigger and twenty years younger than all her Pilates ladies, he didn't blink an eye. How he was the first one to practice every day and the last one to leave. All this stuff that didn't surprise me one tiny bit, although listening kind of killed me because for a second I'd forget Win was lying in a bed a couple doors down, and then when I did, I'd hurt twice as much.

Charlie patted my leg. "Don't worry. It's going to take time, from what I've heard, for Win to get used to all this. He'll come around."

I didn't say anything but I thought to myself, Do you even know my brother? Do you know him at all? Because the way Win was talking in there, it didn't sound like he was going to "come around" anytime soon. When Win was a kid, he had this huge baseball card collection. He still does, in these binders he hasn't looked at in years. But he looked at them a lot when he was a kid, worked on them all the time, and then one day Bill took them down without asking and showed them to a friend, then left them spread out all over the bed, where Win found them. They weren't damaged or anything, although some of the cards were out of their holders, but Win just freaked. He didn't beat Bill up, nothing like that, he just stopped talking to him. And I mean *stopped*. For a whole month. He wouldn't even look at him. If Bill had something Win needed, Win would ask Mom or Dad, or me, even though I was only about six years old and totally blown away by this whole thing. He'd say, "D.J., could you please hand me the glue?" if that happened to be in Bill's hand. Finally he stopped, but for that month, boy, I wasn't the only blown-away one. Bill cried almost every day, and Mom cried too, but Win wouldn't budge. And then of course he didn't call home or talk to us for almost nine months last year . . .

That's the thing. If Win decides not to talk, he can do it pretty much forever. So what if right now he was full of painkillers and in shock and all that. This was still *Win*.

Finally Charlie had to go pick up Bill. I sat by Win's door, wondering if I should tell him that Bill was on his way. It might perk him up. On the other hand, huge flower arrangements kept arriving for him that the nurses just kept at their station because Win had been pretty explicit to them too, about how he felt, and the way he told them off left me not too interested in talking to him, wimp that I am. Instead I just tried to keep people from bothering him like he'd asked me. Which wasn't too hard because this floor was Family Only, so no one came by.

No guests, that is, but all sorts of medical people kept

moving in and out, and then Dr. Rosenberger showed up with a couple young doctors trailing behind him. I was relieved Win didn't yell at *him* at least. He explained he was going to do some tests to see how much Win could feel. Win didn't say okay, but he didn't say no either, so Dr. Rosenberger started poking Win in the leg with this little tool. A pinprick test, he called it. "Just speak up when you feel something."

Win lay there looking at the wall, where the nurses had just rolled him, like he was memorizing the wallpaper.

"How about this?" Dr. Rosenberger asked after a minute, poking him all the time—not hard, but enough that someone would feel it if they had working nerves.

Win still didn't answer, and I started to get a really bad feeling. "Win?" I said. "Please talk to him."

Dr. Rosenberger shot me a look, catching on right away. He leaned right over Win's face. "Listen, Warren"—which no one ever calls Win, ever—"I know this is awful. You have every right to be furious. But we cannot help you—we cannot make you better—without your help. Please, if you feel anything at all, tell me. It is critical that I know."

Win didn't move, didn't even make eye contact. It was like he was in the room alone.

"Win," I pleaded. "Please. For Mom."

Dr. Rosenberger tried a couple more times, but he would have had more luck talking to a rock. Maybe that pinprick was poking Win like a hot needle and it was all he could do not to yell, but I'll never know because he sure wasn't showing anything.

Finally we all left. I must have looked pretty bummed, because out in the hall Dr. Rosenberger took the time to explain to me about the stages of grief, and that it was completely normal for Win to be in denial like this. I nodded, but inside I couldn't help thinking that Win wasn't denying his injury. He was making it his whole entire world, if that makes any sense, and just getting drowned in it without trying to deal with it one tiny bit.

17

BILL

DR. ROSENBERGER ALSO TOLD ME that he'd like to have a family conference call in forty minutes. So I had to give Mom and Dad a heads-up, which meant finding a special cell phone room because heaven forbid you use your phone in the regular hospital rooms, and then oh so luckily right as Mom was asking about Win, I got a second call from BRIAN and so I said Win was doing just what he should be doing—because isn't that what the doctor said, that it was normal not to talk?—and that they'd tell us a whole bunch in the conference, and as fast as I could switched to him.

"Hey."

"Hey. How are you doing out there?" He asked, sounding so concerned.

"Oh, you know . . ." Later I realized I should have apologized right away for my whole *People* mistake. But I didn't, and then by the time I did realize, it didn't matter one way or the other, it was such ancient history, and so irrelevant to what our lives were now.

"No, really. How are *you*? How's Win? Is there anything I can do to help?"

Oh, it was good to hear his voice. It was like the way ice feels on a really bad injury, only warm instead of shivering cold. "You can talk to me," I whispered—whispered because it took so much effort not to bawl. So I probably sounded like I had a bad cold.

"Of course. Whenever you want."

"Okay. How—how was your game on Friday?" Which sounds stupid, but at that moment I really needed to talk about something that wasn't hospitals and spinal cords and all this pain.

Brian laughed like he understood. And he said Hawley lost to Cougar Lake, and then he went into a long description of how on the way home the bus got stopped by a buffalo, because there are a couple buffalo meat farms out that way, and apparently one of the buffalo had got out somehow and was standing in the middle of the road absolutely not interested in letting the bus go by. Jimmy Ott wouldn't let anyone off the bus because he'd been to Yellowstone and seen this video of tourists getting gored by buffalo, stupid tourists videotaping each other getting too close—I remembered that story from Jimmy, and how mad us kids had been that he didn't bring a copy of that video home for us—but eventually this buffalo, the Cougar Lake one, decided he was ready to amble along, like the bus and the honking bus horn and all these football players shouting out the windows had nothing at all to do with his decision.

It was completely hilarious, the way Brian told it, and I laughed so hard my cheeks hurt. And then, just as I was cracking up the most, Charlie walked by the door with Bill, and they both saw me laughing on my cell phone like a heartless moron. So I quick told Brian we'd talk more later and rushed out to hug Bill.

You'd think that, being his sister and all, I'd remember how big Bill is, but each time I see him lately I'm just amazed. Maybe I don't see him that often, or maybe he just keeps bulking up. But it felt so good to put my arms around him and feel all those huge muscles. It made me feel safe. "Charlie here's been filling me in on how smart you are," he said.

"He's lying." I grinned. God, it felt good to have Bill there. Although you could see he was faking that good mood because he had big circles under his eyes like he'd been crying.

We walked down the hall, Charlie staying a bit behind us so that we'd have some privacy. I could see the nurses up and down the hall checking Bill out, and the families too, the moms and sisters. I hoped it would bring Win extra-special care, all those females grooving on Bill like that. Plus Bill was carrying this big pizza box with a big hot-pizza smell.

"How is he? Really?" Bill asked, and all the pain he'd been hiding came out in his voice.

"He's right here," I said, motioning to Win's door.

Bill squared his shoulders and took a deep breath. "Hey there, bro! I brought your favorite."

"You have to lean over him so he can see you," I whispered, kind of angling Bill that way.

He grinned down at Win. "Hey, man. We're going to get you out of here."

Win's eyes flicked over Bill's face for a second. He didn't even look at the pizza box, though the smell was pretty powerful in that little hospital room.

"Hey, Win, you're going to beat this. I just know it."

There was a long silence. Finally Win spoke. "D.J.? Don't you remember my instructions?"

Again, that kicked-in-the-stomach feeling. I tried my best not to gasp, the pain was so strong. As gently as I could, I led Bill back into the hall. He didn't deserve to stay in there and get abused like that.

"He, um . . . Don't take it personally—it's just the stages of grief," I explained. What else could I say? I hoped Bill wouldn't ask me to explain the stages, but he looked too upset, too in shock, to ask anything at all.

There were a couple other doctors and folks at the phone conference besides Dr. Rosenberger, and Charlie of course, and we all sat around this table with a fancy phone thing in the middle. Dr. Rosenberger explained to Mom and Dad the same things he'd said to me, how we really wouldn't know anything for at least another day and maybe several, although the break in the vertebrae looked very clean, which was a good sign, and his spinal cord bruising wasn't that extensive, and how these injuries heal in very different ways and sometimes it takes months for things to happen.

I noticed he didn't mention Win not talking.

"Is he — is he going to walk?" Dad asked, his voice cracking.

"We do not know," Dr. Rosenberger answered in a really no-nonsense way that was actually very reassuring. "We don't know what he's going to be able to do. I can't make any predictions."

Then he said we had other stuff to talk about like rehab, and that there was a great rehab place near Minneapolis we should look into.

Mom asked in a scared voice how much it cost.

Charlie Wright leaned into the table. "That's not something you need to worry about, Linda." Which led to a long discussion about insurance and other financial stuff I wasn't too interested in once I heard we wouldn't be going bankrupt.

Then Dr. Rosenberger said what a great job I was doing, how much it meant to Win.

"I wish I could be there," Mom said, starting to choke up.

"Don't worry, Mom," I said. If Dr. Rosenberger could lie, then so could I. "Win's doing great. You just work on getting yourself better so when you see him, you can give him a big hug." Which was pretty thick, but it seemed to cheer her up. Dr. Rosenberger nodded at me like I'd said the right thing.

Finally the conference call ended, after the doctors recommended a bunch of Web sites so my folks could do that at least. Then everyone cleared out with their piles of papers, and Charlie left too, and it was just me and Bill.

Bill sat there staring at the table. He hadn't said one word, I realized all of a sudden. He hadn't even moved. He looked like a statue. A really sad statue. With big muscles.

"You okay?" I asked.

"It should have been me," he whispered.

I sat on the table next to him. "What are you talking about?"

"It should be me in there, it shouldn't be Win. He doesn't deserve this."

"And *you* do? Come on, Bill—"

He started to cry. "I could handle it better. I don't need football. But it's all he's got."

Bill was right, but I couldn't say that. Also, the very last thing I'd want is Bill hurt. Not that I wanted Win hurt either, but wishing the injury could switch to Bill—not only was it impossible, it was wrong. "He's got us," I said.

Bill snorted. "He's got you. I'm no good at this."

"Me neither," I said, wishing again someone else could step in. I'd been so hopeful about Bill showing up. Now I could see, though, that he wasn't going to be any better at this than me.

⑨ ⑨ ⑨ ⑨

Only Brian Nelson put it a lot differently when we talked that afternoon. We had a really long conversation about Win and Bill, and though I tried not to badmouth either one of them, Brian still got the gist of what was going on.

"You sound really disappointed in Bill," he said, using his family therapist voice.

"Yeah, well, now I feel like I've got *two* brothers to take care of." And no one to take care of me, though I didn't say that out loud. It sounded bad enough already.

"That's really rough." There was this little pause. "Isn't Bill younger than Win?"

"Yeah! But so am I. And Bill's older than *me*."

"But . . . isn't it different?"

"No!" Although it was. I could see what Brian was getting at. Because Win has always been such a big brother to Bill, bossing him around when they were kids, and then I guess again today when he blew off Bill's pizza and kicked him out. Bill's always been happy-go-lucky, but that attitude doesn't work so well in a situation like this. Kind of like Dad and needles. It's just not in him.

Not that I thought that all out on the phone. But Brian planted the seed.

"You know," Brian said, "my mom—I was talking to her about this, I hope that's okay, and she said some people are just amazing, people who are hurt like this. They decide from the get-go to get better. And some people take a while."

"The stages of grief," I said, glad I had something to add. Brian's mom is a family therapist herself, that's why he's so good at talking—all the time us Schwenk kids were milking cows, he was learning how to talk.

"Yeah. And it sounds like you're doing the right thing by just waiting."

That was nice. Even though I felt like I couldn't be any more useless if I had my thumb stuck up my nose. We talked a bit more about stuff that wasn't quite so heavy, a movie he said I really needed to see, which was fun to hear, normal life talk, and we hung up.

Then I checked my messages. I had one from Kyle Jorgensen, who I didn't even know had my number, and Amber asking what she and Dale could do, and other people as well asking to help. But I didn't call any of them back because I didn't know what to say. Even if Amber and those other folks were here in Seattle, even if they were standing right next to me, I wouldn't know how they could help. Because if Win wasn't going to talk, no one could help him, not one little bit.

When I got back to Win's room, Bill and Charlie were chatting with a nurse who was holding Bill's pizza box like she was a waitress or something. "I'll see if I can find a haz mat fridge," she said, grinning at Bill, who grinned back because grinning at girls just comes naturally to him, and then she walked past me with a big thumbs-up sign.

"What was that all about?" I asked, though the flirting part was pretty clear to me already.

"Win just ate half a pizza," Charlie said proudly, "though I don't see how. That kind of seasoning would just go right through me."

"Well, you know Win," Bill added, shaking his head. He looked pretty proud too, which I guess he had a right to be considering it was his idea to pick up the pizza in the first place. Win's special pizza was made of broccoli and pineapple and anchovies and those little hot peppers from Mexico that burn my tongue right off. You see, Win figured out pretty early in college that when you order a pizza, everyone comes around asking for a slice, so he started getting pizzas with the most disgusting ingredients he could think of so that other people wouldn't snag it all. And guess what, people didn't because they're not insane, and then he actually developed a taste for that combination and now that's all he'll eat.

Anyway, while I had been on my cell phone talking to Brian, that nurse asked Win if he was hungry, and it turns out that one of the feelings you have left after a spinal cord injury is hunger, and Win couldn't help but admit that he was. So the nurse offered him some of Bill's pizza and he said yes, and then she cut it into little bits and fed it to him with a fork. Apparently Win wouldn't even look at her as she fed him. He just kept his eyes closed, and the only words he said were "I don't want any more." And when she offered to save the rest for later, he didn't answer. But at least he ate, which I guess merits a thumbs-up sign even if the way he ate was incredibly rude.

So that was extremely good news, that Win still had a taste for hot peppers and broccoli, only that evening when Bill asked if he'd like the rest of the pizza, Win wouldn't answer. He wouldn't answer any of us. We talked to the nurse about it—the same one, thank goodness, so she knew what was going on—and she just sighed, and microwaved the pizza and brought it in all cut up, not saying a word, and sat down next to Win and fed him without even asking if it was okay. And Win ate, again not looking at her or acknowledging her in any way, and when it was all finished and she asked if he'd like anything else, and then asked if he had any special requests for breakfast, he acted like she didn't exist. So in the end Win's eating wasn't really such good news at all.

Charlie and Bill and I stayed outside Win's room until it got really late, discussing this and going through the hospital menu trying to figure out what Win might want for breakfast, then Charlie drove us back to his house. The next day we sat outside Win's room again. Bill went in first thing to say hello, but Win ignored him no matter what he said, and Bill came back out wiping his eyes and went into that little conference room all by himself so he could cry without anyone seeing. I tried to speak to Win as well, and he ignored me just as completely. It's amazing how much someone can ignore you when they can't even move. But it didn't seem to bother me as much as it did Bill. Maybe I was used to it. Or maybe, I don't know, my feelings weren't as hurt.

So the nurses got stuck feeding Win his silent-treatment breakfast, and then when they came back for his silent-treatment lunch, Charlie took Bill and me down to the hospital cafeteria to get us away for a bit. The three of us didn't talk much. Charlie wasn't saying that Win would snap out of it anymore. Then as we were settling into this pie that had seen better days, Charlie asked Bill his opinion of Minnesota's chances.

Bill pushed his pie around and shrugged. "It doesn't matter." Meaning it wasn't right for us to talk football with Win so hurt.

But you know, Bill loves football. He doesn't have Win's intensity—if you met Bill you'd think he was just a big guy squeaking by. But you don't get his kind of muscles just squeaking by, you get them sweating your guts out for years. And you don't start Big Ten football as a sophomore unless you're out there every day giving three hundred percent. Which Bill does, but he makes it look easy. Maybe he bends a little better—bends emotionally, if you know what I mean, because he doesn't have to fight everything, including Dad, the way Win does. And it wasn't fair that Win was taking away Bill's love of football—taking it away so much that Bill wished he was hurt instead. That wasn't right.

"Yeah, it does matter," I said. "Because I think Minnesota's got a real shot at the title next year." Which at least got Bill talking a little, and somehow led to a discussion of 3-4 versus 4-3 defense, with examples of how 3-4 was actually better than most people recognized, and Charlie even used some grapes to lay out a couple plays. Which might not be a good idea — not the grapes, but them talking — seeing as Minnesota might end up playing Washington someday if both of them happen to make it to the Rose Bowl, although to be realistic this will happen just a couple days before hell freezes over.

Then we went back upstairs, and Bill and I called home. Only Mom was so upset that she couldn't really talk. We ended up just reassuring her about how Win was sleeping so much that she'd be wasting her time out here, and Dad too.

"Jeez," Bill said when we got off the phone. "She needs more help than Win does."

I nodded, and we went back to our chairs. Bill and Charlie got to talking about next week's Minnesota game, and Charlie mentioned that a coach had called him, a coach who'd had a player with SCI, and that coach said it was really important to get the other players back out on the field. And he didn't mean just physically.

Which also gave me something to think about.

Finally, when it was clear Win was done for the night except for the nurses rolling him every two hours so he wouldn't get bedsores, and adjusting his machinery and stuff, we left.

We sat around the Wrights' kitchen for a long while, Marla making cocoa and asking questions about Win until it was clear that our answers were just bumming everyone out.

"You know," I said, breaking the silence finally, "I think Bill needs to go home."

"Hey!" Bill said at once.

I'd already blown it, on the very first line. "Just—just listen, okay? Win's not talking, and you know him. He could keep this up forever. And it just seems like a waste having us both here when Mom's at home needing all the help she can get. Win doesn't need you right now. But he's going to need you"—my voice broke a little—"he's going to need you for the rest of his life."

Marla came over and squeezed my shoulders. Actually, she started giving me a back rub, which felt so darn good—she's got strong hands for a skinny lady. Maybe Pilates does that too.

"I can't leave him," Bill said.

"You're not leaving him," I said. "You're going to Mom. And Dad, too. He's a basket case. And I really think you should try to play on Saturday."

"It would mean so much to your teammates," Marla chipped in. Which was pretty clever of her, dropping that ace in like that.

And you know what? In the end, Bill agreed.

☉ ☉ ☉ ☉

That night I lay awake in Marla's guest bed for a long while. Secretly—even though I'd never, ever, say this out loud—I thought I was handling things a lot better than Bill was. He and Win were so close that I wasn't sure he could step out of being a little brother and become a pretend mom instead. Not that I could, but I felt I had a little bit better shot at it, at least until Mom was well enough to do it herself.

And there was another thing I hadn't said either, mainly because if I did I would have started crying. But you know how I told Brian that I felt like I was taking care of two brothers? Well, I'd come to Seattle to help Win, and now it turned out that I might not be able to, not until he turned it around. But at least I could help Bill. I was asking Bill to go home because I loved him too much to keep him here.

18

My Own Personal Time Zone

THE NEXT MORNING, OF COURSE, I was kicking myself. Sure, it's great to be self-sacrificing at midnight, but when I saw Charlie drive Bill away—after Bill came up to say goodbye to Win, who ignored him—I was having some extremely serious second thoughts. But by then it was too late.

And it wasn't like Win said to himself that maybe now that D.J. was alone she might be worth talking to, or worth helping with the whole feeding business. But I couldn't leave, because I'd volunteered for this. Volunteered twice, actually— in the airport with Dad, and then over hot cocoa with Bill when I must have lost my brain for a minute. Plus three or four times a day I had to call Mom and Dad, and Bill, fill them in on everything that was going on. I could tell from Mom and Dad's questions that Bill had skipped a bunch of details about Win that would have upset them too much, instead he took what I'd said to him and turned it around a bit, telling Mom it was a lot more important for her to be with Win in rehab, and for the rest of his life, than at this minute. Which I know helped her a lot.

Besides, the hospital folks were talking about sending Win to rehab in the next few days, which I thought they were doing because they couldn't figure out what else to do with him, but it turns out that a bunch of patients get moved just a week or two after they're injured because it's so important to start rehab right away. So Mom flying all the way out to Washington State wouldn't be all that productive.

Still, she and Dad asked everything they could, including questions I couldn't really answer, like whether he could feel anything, because Win still wouldn't even tell the doctors when he could feel pinpricks. One time Dr. Rosenberger got on his case and Win started jerking his head around, he was so angry, and they had to sedate him.

I didn't tell Mom and Dad about that. I didn't tell them everything I was learning about spinal cord injuries, like how they turn you into a baby again — even the folks with really incomplete injuries get turned into babies for a while, and I'm not talking about the feeding. The nurses did their best to hide it from me — not *hide,* but just make it clear that I wasn't supposed to be on diaper duty. Although they explained that it was a huge part of rehab, figuring all that out, which really made rehab something to look forward to. Instead when I called home I told them that Win was eating a lot, which he was — Charlie was bringing in one of those special pizzas every day for Win to chow down on silently — and that really seemed to cheer them up.

When I wasn't talking to Mom and Dad, I spent most of

my time sitting in the hall by Win's door feeling pretty blue. Whenever something beeped in his room, I'd check on it—I was getting pretty good at resetting IV pumps and stuff— and I could help the nurses roll Win every two hours like we were supposed to, not even irritating my shoulder that much. Otherwise I just sat.

After a few days in that hall, though, I got pretty tired of the stares from other families, and the nurses too, and with- out even really thinking about it, I stood up and dragged my chair into Win's room, off to the side where I wouldn't be in anyone's way.

Win didn't say a word. Didn't even act like he noticed. Finally after about an hour, I guess he couldn't stand it any- more. "Get out."

"I can't."

"Why not?"

I gave him the only answer that made sense to me. "Because I'm your sister."

I guess he couldn't think of anything to say back to this— it's not like he could deny it or anything. So he didn't say any- thing more, and there I sat, hour after hour, staring at all the machinery. Then I'd go do one of my phone calls, or listen in on the doctors' conferences, or talk to Win's shrink.

Which was something else I hadn't planned on, spending time with this lady with clothes like I'd never seen that looked really boring but expensive. Dr. Rosenberger brought her in once it was clear that Win, you know, had *issues,* but of course he wasn't talking, and all those machines they ran him through to look at his spine and brain and skeleton weren't so good at looking at his mind. So I got stuck being the Win-mind interpreter.

She'd take me into a little room — the room where I'd first talked to Dr. Rosenberger, or to other floors, which was like going to another country, those floors were so different from ours — and ask questions with these huge silences, so huge that I *had* to talk, and it turns out that sometimes you can say things to a stranger you could never say to your family or your neighbors, especially in Red Bend. Plus she acted like everything I said was just amazingly interesting. Especially the fight between Dad and Win.

I'd brought it up just to explain how good Win is at not talking but the psychia-lady kept asking how it started, which was Dad questioning whether Win was good enough to go pro and whether he'd inherit the farm. She went over this for a full hour until I felt really empty, and I had to ask her not to tell anyone. She said she couldn't because it was against the law, which gave me something to chew over, imagining her getting her hair cut and mentioning the Schwenk family and the police busting through the door to handcuff her.

There wasn't a whole lot to think about, most of the time.

She liked the baseball card story too, and the fact that Win is all about football. And she had me talk up another storm about Bill and why he'd left Seattle, which she seemed to feel was a bad thing until she heard my side of the story, and then she agreed that helping Mom and Dad was probably just as important as helping Win, and that my wanting to protect Bill said a lot. Only, I realized later, she never told me what it said, and we ran out of time before I ever got a chance to ask.

There were some things I never mentioned to the psychia-lady because they were way too personal. Like how I'd stay late at night—Charlie Wright found me a car somewhere, one of the amazing things he and Marla did—and I'd sit next to Win's bed, the lights all dim. I'd be really quiet and after a while maybe he forgot I was there, and he'd start crying. It was so awful, especially because I couldn't imagine crying like that—I'd want to curl up and be able to wipe my tears at least, and my nose.

The first time I sat there frozen, and then I couldn't stand it anymore and I came over with a tissue and dried his tears. And then I did something I remember from being a kid. I held the tissue to his nose and said, "Blow," and maybe he was desperate or maybe he didn't care or maybe even he was grateful, but he did, and he cried some more as I stayed with him, and then I went back to my chair and after a while he fell asleep and I left.

The next night the same thing happened, and the night af-ter that. We never talked about it—he'd have died if I brought it up, and vice versa—but it changed things, just a hair, between us.

⑨ ⑨ ⑨ ⑨

So it turned out I was okay at some things but really awful at others, like the tons of cards Win got from all over the country. It wasn't like he wanted to read them, stories about SCI patients who sounded just like the ticket lady's cousin, or "we're praying for you" stuff that was nice for them but I sure wasn't seeing God's Work here in the hospital, and don't tell me God was there with Win's boogers because that was me alone.

Luckily Marla Wright—*that's* where God was, with her and Charlie—took over, and got her Pilates ladies to open the letters and save the money that was in them sometimes, and write thank-you notes to the really personal ones like the guy who typed using a stick strapped to his forehead and a manual typewriter because he'd been hurt before computers and he liked his way better, and he wanted to tell Win he was going to be okay. That one they showed me, and I saved it. A real typed letter—I'd never seen one of those. And they helped with the flowers that kept on coming, even found a nursing home where the folks were just so pleased to get them.

It wasn't just flowers either. All Win's buddies from the team and from school, friends from his business classes, wanted to come by. Which is what friends do, and any person in their right mind would want to see them. But Win made it pretty clear that he wouldn't tolerate one second of friendship, which broke my heart a little bit—I mean, it would have broken my heart if I'd had any heart still left to break. Instead Charlie got stuck telling all of them, as nicely as he could I'm sure, that Win just wanted to be alone.

Reporters kept trying to get to Win too. There was no way I was going to say one word to those bums, not after *People*, and it wasn't like Win was itching for a press conference. Charlie did a super job, saying we'd talk when we were ready but that right now we needed our privacy. And reporters are just like little kids quarreling — if you don't talk back eventually they give up. Although I was always careful to leave the hospital by a back entrance in case someone was waiting with a couple questions, or a camera, which I would have broken, so they're lucky they weren't.

One thing I did do, once I got to know the nurses, was sign their *People* magazines. Which they were very nice about, and some of them actually went out and hunted down extra copies even though the issue had changed. Now I felt a bit stupid getting so upset about that article considering what I was grappling with now. And to tell you the truth, the picture actually wasn't so bad, in a girl-in-sports-bra way. At least I wasn't cross-eyed, which I'm so good at whenever there's a camera around.

The nurses were great, maybe because they'd seen how cute Bill is but I don't think so. They didn't seem to mind when Win ignored them or told them to leave. They said that was just part of their job, which I really appreciated, and a couple times I almost said something sharp to Win about how he could thank them just once for keeping him alive. But that was the whole point, I think. He didn't want to be alive.

Which Dr. Rosenberger and the psychia-lady and Mom and Dad and I got to talk about the day before Win got transferred to rehab—that rehab hospital in Minnesota the doctor had recommended—that Win didn't want to be alive anymore.

I couldn't help but point out that it's hard to kill yourself when you can't move.

"You'd be surprised," Dr. Rosenberger said really quietly, which set Mom crying and me kicking myself for opening my big fat mouth.

It turns out rehab is just like football—although he didn't put it like that, I added that now—in that a huge part is mental, and if you've got a good attitude you're going to do a lot better. He had books on people with SCI who ride horses and run marathons—or roll them, I guess—and do pretty much everything except walk on the moon. I couldn't read them, though, because the contrast between those folks and Win depressed me too much. And Dr. Rosenberger said people who want to die get their way sooner or later. Like this cow we had once with really bad ankles, although I just added that too. Dr. Rosenberger doesn't know about her.

Then Mom said it was killing her not to be with her son, and she had to come out, just to be with him as he flew back if nothing else.

"Linda, I completely understand," Dr. Rosenberger said. "But it's more important that you be at the rehab hospital, get oriented before he arrives. That will really help get him stabilized."

Which even she agreed was a good idea, and I was at least tactful enough not to say that "stabilized" was a total joke because Win was so far from being stable.

We flew back to our own time zone on a private medical jet, paid for by the university or someone that definitely wasn't us, a nurse working on Win full-time as I sat watching. I couldn't help but think how much this must be costing, and how much the farm could use that money in a hundred different ways. Not that I wanted anything less for Win—it wasn't that at all—but still, it's hard not to notice the contrast between us skimping along on nothing, and this. It makes you think.

Mom and Dad had driven over from Red Bend that morning, Dad leaving the cows with those two nice farmers and watching through his rearview mirror the whole way out, I'm sure. Mom rode lying down in the back of the Caravan but she was still on painkillers so I don't think it bothered her too much, she was so anxious to see Win. The university had found them a little apartment near the hospital that some charity offers to families like ours. Once Mom was established in the rehab hospital and the little apartment, taking over the mothering responsibilities from me, Dad would return to the farm. Then we would all take turns helping Mom out.

Bill came as well. He'd gone back to school for a few days and had even suited up for the game on Saturday, though he didn't play because he'd missed so many practices. At least people applauded when he came on the field, because of Win and all.

They were there when we got to our floor, all three of them. I was in the back of the elevator as the nurse and orderly rolled out Win, still pretty sedated from the trip, and I could see the shock on Mom and Dad's faces as they realized for the first time just how bad off he was.

"Oh, baby," Mom said, her whole face collapsing.

Win had his eyes closed although I couldn't believe he was asleep. But I just explained to Mom and Dad everything the nurses were doing as we followed them into the room, what all the equipment was and what the beeping meant, all of us ignoring the real issue, that Win was lying there with a broken neck not even acknowledging his parents.

There was a conference scheduled with his new doctors and nurses and physical therapy folks, the PTs, to fill Mom and Dad in on everything. Mom asked if I wanted to be there, but from the way she sounded—I don't want to put words in her mouth or anything, maybe she was just tired and hurting from her back—well, I couldn't help but think that maybe she felt Win's not talking was my fault. Or not my *fault* but that she'd do a better job, being his mom and all. Which I was absolutely ready to agree with, every bit. So I said I didn't think I'd be much help in that meeting and maybe I better just head home. And I grabbed my dirty clothes and toothbrush and deodorant and hit the road back to Red Bend. Dad was hoping I'd get there in time for evening milking with the farmers, and Mom was hoping I could make Curtis dinner, but frankly I didn't care about either of those things. I just wanted to be *gone.*

19

EVEN MORE FAMILY TROUBLE

I SPENT THE FIRST HALF-HOUR in the Caravan screaming, trying to get out my frustration at how awful this whole thing was, every single part and every single person. It was such a great sound after all those days of silence and whispering and tiptoeing around. Then, pretty hoarse, I called Brian.

Brian and I had talked almost every day I was in Seattle. Sometimes he'd just tell me about his day, how football was going, which I have to say I felt a bit different about now because of Win getting injured and also because my life was so far from being in the sunshine working out. Although Hawley and Red Bend were tied for first and it looked like they might actually meet in the playoffs. I couldn't help but notice that in the end my separated shoulder didn't even matter seeing as I still would have had to quit football because of Win. Although you have to stop those what-if thoughts before they take over your brain.

Other times I'd go through my day, doing my best not to complain, though given the situation it was hard not to. Brian couldn't have been more sympathetic. He'd agree that it sounded tough, and tell me I was doing as good a job as anyone (which apparently Mom didn't agree with, but so what), and that these things take time. And say how much people in school were talking about Win, and how impressed everyone was that I was helping him. Even Brian's friends — his jerk friends, although he didn't call them that and I didn't point it out — said I was pretty amazing to be doing something like this. Which I have to admit helped a bit, hearing that.

He had even offered to drive over and meet me at the rehab hospital. Which was incredibly great of him but I said no, because I didn't want him seeing Win for one thing, and because it looked like I'd be heading home soon, and now I was. I took the Caravan, seeing as Mom and Dad didn't need a car because they were close enough to the hospital to walk, and I sure couldn't walk to Red Bend.

"Can we get together tonight?" I asked Brian now, so desperate for some company that wasn't in hospital clothes.

"Aw, I've got this calculus exam — my mom'll kill me if I leave the house."

I grinned. "How can she kill you if you're gone?"

Brian laughed. "Psychic death rays, duh. But how about tomorrow, right after practice?"

Which sounded great to me, and then he had to go study calculus, and I was grateful that at least I didn't have to do *that,* and I called Amber. Who I'd been talking to as well, only she wasn't as great as Brian because she kept getting mad at Win. And then I'd have to defend him, and get off the phone feeling twice as guilty about not being nicer about him. So instead we'd talk about her job search, and how annoying it was to sleep on a foldout bed at Dale's friend's apartment, and whether she should go to beauty school.

That's what we talked about now, beauty school and haircutting and how she'd love to put highlights in my hair if I'd let her, which I said I would once she learned how, and for long stretches of that conversation I'd forget that Amber wasn't in Red Bend anymore, and it wasn't until after my cell phone died that I remembered she was gone.

I got home in time for milking even though those two farmers were okay without me, hurrah. The farm looked so rusty and grimy and broken down, such a contrast to the shiny hospital rooms and the Wrights' brand new house. It was like a slap in the face, a fresh one, about our lack of money. Although at least those two nice farmers were working for free.

At dinner Curtis hardly said a word. "So, how's school?" I asked finally.

He jumped. "Nothing. Um, Mr. Larson's mom died."

"Oh." I didn't know Mr. Larson had a mom—still had one, I mean. Curtis didn't say anything more. He didn't even ask about Win, which was good because I was sick of talking about it. He just slunk off to his room looking worried as I tried to find space for the leftovers in the fridge between all the casseroles people had been bringing, and then I took a long bath, which I don't normally do but it was pretty much heaven after all that hospital air, and went to bed knowing that tomorrow I'd have a big day of rest, no milking or school, or going into town to get stared at. Besides, after missing a week of school—because that's how long I'd been gone, which seems amazing since I felt like I'd been gone years and years, but it turned out they moved Win to rehab only eight days after his injury—well, it wasn't like one more day was going to make much difference one way or the other. Instead I'd sleep in and enjoy a little bit of my own personal time zone.

I even brought Smut up with me because I'd missed her as much as anything, even more than she missed me, which is saying something, and she was thrilled to be on my bed enjoying my own personal time zone with me.

I didn't set the alarm of course, but I heard Curtis get up. Even though he was tiptoeing around, I still woke up because of my early-morning genes and all. He must have heard me rustling because he hollered, "Don't worry! I'm okay," which was really great of him, and I settled back with Smut, listening to the farmers' trucks arrive to milk, which was like a lullaby putting me to sleep.

Smut woke me a few hours later needing to go out, and I brought coffee to the farmers, who were just finishing up, and they were just as grateful for the coffee as I was for them.

Walking back to the house, something seemed off somehow, and then I realized: the pickup was missing. It's usually parked right next to the barn door, under a bit of overhang so you won't get wet, but there wasn't anything there at the moment but gravel and some dead weeds.

No wonder Curtis didn't want me getting up with him, not if I'd catch him taking the pickup to school. Which is just a teensy bit of a bad idea seeing as Curtis is only fourteen. Jeez, I'm home for less than a day and already he's pulling stuff he'd *never* do with Mom and Dad around. But just because he hates riding the bus doesn't mean he can take the pickup, which I might need for one thing, not to mention it's completely illegal. Sure, we know a couple Red Bend cops from the Jorgensens' picnic but he'd still get a warning at least if he got caught.

I thought about this, making myself a big non-hospital-food breakfast. I even thought about calling the school, or driving down there, but that would just make things worse. Better to talk it out over dinner, let him know I wasn't going to put up with that sort of behavior no matter how much the bus sucks. Besides, starting tomorrow I'd be driving him to school again when I bit the bullet and went back myself. So I just left the dishes piled up in the sink because who was going to complain about it, and instead I went out and shot some hoops.

Holding that basketball . . . wow, it felt *good*. Not in a

Brian-Nelson's-back-muscles kind of way, but not that far off. It's a pretty great rush, sinking a three-pointer. Which I did once and then my shoulder gave a twinge because it turns out that shooting really aggravates a mostly healed Type I separation.

So even though that twinge was super tiny, I decided not to push things seeing as basketball season was starting soon, and instead I did a whole bunch of shooting with my left hand. Which was fun too, because of all the Horse I'd played—this game where you take turns shooting tough shots, and I used to play left-handed with Curtis when he was little to make it more fair—and also I had this art teacher once who said that drawing with your other hand "opens your mind," though I'm so bad at art that she could have opened my mind with a backhoe and it wouldn't have helped. But maybe shooting left-handed opened my mind a bit. Who knows. It opened it enough that I actually started thinking that maybe going back to school wouldn't be so bad, not if I could play basketball. Then I remembered how Brian and I were getting together after football practice, and that opened my mind even more.

Just then the phone rang, and I got it just in time. It was Curtis. "Hey," he whispered, sounding worse than panicked. "Could you—could you give me a jump?"

Which was just great. Curtis takes the pickup and of

course the battery dies. "Couldn't you ask someone there?" I asked.

There was a long silence. No, Curtis couldn't. He can't talk in the best of situations. Plus he was underage. If word got out . . .

I sighed. "Okay. Where are you?" So much for my big mind-opening day of rest.

Another long silence. Curtis mumbled something. He tried again. "Eau Claire."

"*Eau Claire?* You're kidding."

"I—I've got the address." I could hear him speaking to someone else—a girl.

"Who's that with you?" I asked.

"Um, Sarah. Listen, the address is—"

"You're with *Sarah?* You drove the pickup to *Eau Claire* with *Sarah Zorn?*"

"The address is . . ." He gave me a street I'd never heard of, of course, and a number, and I wrote them down but I sure didn't register them because I was so in shock.

I was in shock for a big chunk of the drive too, heading to Eau Claire at eighty miles an hour so my little brother wouldn't get arrested for cutting school and driving underage. Then the shock kind of wore off enough for me to get angry. To get furious. What the heck was he thinking? Taking the pickup to school, that's understandable — once. But joy riding to a city two hours away, cutting school with your girlfriend? Plus stealing a truck—is it stealing when the truck belongs to your dad? Is it stealing when the truck is dead?

Damn. Even Bill wouldn't have pulled a stunt like this, not in eighth grade. Curtis had always seemed so levelheaded. Weird as heck, yeah, with his skull collection and his chess-playing girlfriend, but I never would have thought he'd do this. Curtis hadn't really gotten in trouble for sleeping over at Sarah's. I guess Mom figured her blowing her back out was punishment enough—it sure *seemed* like it was. But I guess not, not if Curtis was now doing something ten times worse. Only I couldn't even call Mom to tell her what had happened, ask her what to do because, duh, I'd forgotten my cell phone. Left it on the counter charging, which was incredibly brilliant but it's not like I didn't have a number of other things on my mind as I was racing out of the house, things about my little brother the felon.

I got to Eau Claire at last, and then I had to ask a guy at the gas station for directions, which he didn't know although you'd think gas station guys would, but a guy filling up his car helped me out, and then I had to stop this lady walking her dog and ask again—both times just about dying because asking for directions isn't one of my greatest skills—and finally I got to the street number Curtis had said, but I must have written it down wrong or he said it wrong, which was more likely, because it was a huge middle school. Which is not where most kids go joy riding to, right?

Only there was the pickup, sticking out like a sore thumb on the side of the road. Right next to a NO PARKING—FIRE LANE sign. Another law he'd broken. And Curtis wasn't anywhere in sight.

I was so furious that I almost blew out the Caravan's tires, I backed into the curb so hard turning around. I got the jumper cables out of the truck because it's not like this is the first time the battery died, and got it jumped all by myself, not a soul in sight and me with steam coming out of my ears, I was so angry. At least the truck started right up. And at least there was a note under the windshield saying the battery was dead and they were waiting for a jump. In girl handwriting— probably Sarah. Who also wasn't around, not that I'd been counting on her help, but still.

I couldn't believe Curtis. Could not believe him. To call me on my big day of rest, make me drive all the way to Eau Claire, and then not even *wait* for me? Maybe he was hiding somewhere, like I was in the mood for *that*. He certainly wasn't in the parking lot, though if he had been, wandering around slashing tires, I wouldn't have been a bit surprised.

Just then someone walked out of the building, and all this noise poured out of the gym—you could tell it was a gym just from the way it was shaped—and I raced up and grabbed the door before it shut. Maybe Curtis was in there. In fact, he'd be pretty lucky if he *was* in the gym because that meant I couldn't kill him, not until we got outside.

Only he wasn't, or at least I didn't see him and he's really easy to pick out because he's so tall. There were kids everywhere making that enormous ear-bending racket you always get in gyms, and tables holding booths with flowers turned a couple different colors, and water soaking through different materials, and robots being displayed by kids who looked like robot builders . . . A science fair. Great. Right in front of me people jostled around one booth, and through the racket I heard, "That is so totally disgusting" in that tone people use when they can't stop looking, and then someone moved and I could read the sign, really neat computer printing, DESICCA-TION AND ITS EFFECTS, and then someone else moved and—

Remember back a zillion years ago when the milk house roof got smashed? And I found a bunch of dried-up rats that Curtis took away like they were diamonds or something? Well, here they were. Only now they were in little glass boxes, the kind you see in a museum, one in each box, or rat parts in some of them. And next to each box was a little paragraph in that same nice computer printing, and arrows going to one thing, like teeth or hair, or their dried-up skinny bald tails. It was the sort of exhibit you didn't even want to look at, and then once you started, you couldn't stop.

20

THINGS ARE LOOKING BETTER—
NO, I TAKE THAT BACK

ACTUALLY, IT TOOK ME a couple minutes to realize these were Schwenk Farm rats. At first I could see only that they were rats that had been all dried out, which rang a little bell in my memory because as you know I have some experience with that kind of rodent. Then I worked my way close enough to see the little rat bodies, which looked a *lot* like the rats I'd seen, and then as I went over each little description I happened to come across the words BY SARAH ZORN AND CURTIS SCHWENK, and I even thought to myself how bizarre this was because I had a brother with that exact same name, and it wasn't until I got to RED BEND MIDDLE SCHOOL that it really began to sink in that this was Curtis's handiwork.

My anger—it was like it had been sucked up by a vacuum cleaner or something. Now all I felt was amazed. And slowly this other feeling just bubbling up inside me—proud. Proud and happy. He wasn't cutting school at all, not if he was here at a science fair—that's as school as you can get. And he wasn't joy riding—he'd just needed the pickup to carry the booth. Sure, he was driving underage, which wasn't so smart, but my brother wasn't a felon lawbreaker at all.

Just then a couple kids started whispering, "It's them, it's them!" and there were Curtis and Sarah walking up, both pink with embarrassment, holding—ready for this?—a trophy.

Curtis saw me and his pink embarrassment turned to white-faced fear. "I'm sorry—I meant to wait out there . . . they made me come in—"

"This is *awesome*," I said. "I can't believe you did this."

Curtis gulped, and then slowly managed a smile. "Yeah, Sarah has a laser printer."

"That's not what I meant—" I began, but right at that moment they were mobbed by folks asking them questions, wanting their picture in front of the booth.

Anyway, it turns out Curtis and Sarah came in third, which really ticked me off because their exhibit was *so* much better than anything else there, and so much more popular. But the winners were this kid who built a refrigerator "by himself" even though his dad owns an air-conditioning business so you can imagine, and a girl who recorded all these bird songs and made little charts of them, don't ask me how, and had the charts up and the recordings going and you had no idea what it meant but it obviously took her a huge amount of time.

We packed the rat display into the back of the Caravan because I didn't want it getting jostled in the truck, and luckily the truck still started and I gave Curtis my best imitation-

Mom lecture about driving safely because he'd get arrested if he got caught, and they followed me out.

Only before we even got on the highway I pulled into a pancake house because I was totally ravenous and because we needed to celebrate that third place trophy. Sarah ate a ton of food, which I would never have predicted, though not as much as I did, or Curtis who doesn't have a hollow leg, he's just plain hollow. The waitress was impressed, even. And I found out the whole story, though getting information out of the two of them was a bit like dentistry to tell you the truth, how Curtis skipped practice to buy the Plexiglas and then stayed up all night with Sarah arranging those dried-up bodies, Mr. Larson helping them out and keeping their secret, which is just one of the things that makes him an amazing teacher. He was supposed to drive them to Eau Claire but then his mom died, which is why Curtis had to take the pickup and Sarah and the display because he was too scared to ask another teacher, or me, for a ride. Too scared to let on about the science fair.

"The guys would make cracks," he said. "And Dad. You know . . ."

I had a little pang when I realized I was one of the people Curtis was afraid of. I'd already teased him even, last fall, pointing out how gross the rats were. "Forget about Dad," I said. "I'll take care of him." I meant it too. It was the least I could do.

I paid for lunch with all the cash I had, and Curtis and Sarah chipped in, which I very much appreciated, and we managed an okay tip with all the change we could find behind the Caravan cushions, and then we bought gas with Mom's credit card, which I'm only supposed to use in emergencies, which I considered being stuck in Eau Claire to be.

Then, totally stuffed, we set out for Red Bend at an extremely legal rate of speed, and I finally had some down time to collect my thoughts, and then my heart did a midair somersault because I remembered Brian. In all this Eau Claire rat drama, that one extremely exciting fact actually slipped my mind. Now, though, I could barely wait. I spent most of the drive getting more and more psyched. Brian would bust a gut about Curtis. He'd barely believed it last summer, Curtis driving Dad around after his hip transplant, and the notion of Curtis heading to a city with a *girl* for a science fair — that was pretty amazing. Although I'd stress the not-teasing part, just so you know.

From the way dusk was falling, I could tell that football practice was due to end soon. Then Brian and I could just sit in a car and talk the way Amber and I used to, or go to the movies. Or he could help with the evening milking for all I cared. Whatever he wanted, I was up for it. I'd meet him anywhere. Which of course might be a bit difficult to arrange seeing as I didn't have my cell phone. But there were other options.

We drove our Schwenk convoy straight to Sarah's house, parking the pickup around the corner so no one could see who'd been driving, and I rang the doorbell holding the trophy, Curtis pretty nervous because her folks haven't cared much for him since the basement incident. But when her mom answered—pretty mad about seeing her daughter with that troublemaker—I explained what they'd really been doing (skipping the part about the pickup, duh), and Mrs. Zorn was so shocked, and then so pleased, that she came out to the Caravan to see the exhibit, Paul right behind her just amazed I was at his house, and they both had that reaction I was getting used to, a barfing face followed by real curiosity.

So Curtis went from being Troublemaker to Good Guy again, and Mrs. Zorn invited us in for some ice cream, and I said I'd love to but I had to run an errand, and would it be okay if Curtis hung out there for a few hours? And she said of course, and Curtis and Sarah looked even happier if that was possible, and I took off for Hawley.

If you'd told me way back in September that D.J. Schwenk would be driving up to Hawley High School as cool as a cucumber, I'd have told you to go get your head examined. But after everything I'd been through these past few months, the whole Red Bend–Hawley rivalry seemed just a little tiny bit pathetic. Besides, Brian had said even his friends said good things about me. Not that I lay awake nights worrying about their opinion of me or anything, but it had to help Brian, hearing that.

Hawley High School is a lot newer than Red Bend, which you'd expect given our two towns, and its football stands were a lot bigger and nicer-looking. Practice was already over, and I panicked for a second until I saw Brian's Cherokee in the parking lot still. I pulled up nearby, admiring the stars and wondering what the two of us would say after hello. Whether we'd make out a bit. Not that I'd driven over for that, but I wouldn't, you know, turn it down.

A group of guys came out of the gym, hard to see in the twilight, only I heard Brian's laugh and I knew he was in the crowd. They ambled toward the parking lot and I got out of the Caravan, nervous now because I wasn't exactly sure how to act with all those guys around, and wishing I'd been able to call Brian first. Plus I couldn't help thinking how crappy the Caravan looked next to all those cars the football players drove. Not that they all drove cars as new as Brian's, but they were all a lot newer than mine.

The guys got closer and now I could make out Brian, his hair so shiny the way it always is. He turned in my direction and all of a sudden he saw me. He had this little start of recognition, and then his mouth dropped open. Not in surprise. In shock. In total, what-the-hell-is-*she*-doing-here shock.

21

Wanted: A Town Full of Strangers

For one instant, Brian and I stared at each other—him with that shocked face and me with my heart basically stopped—and a few of the guys caught sight of me and froze, looking back and forth between me and Brian while he didn't do a thing. Then I climbed into the Caravan and drove off.

Which wasn't quite the exit I was looking for because the Caravan has some exhaust issues and it backfired a couple times, which is something you never see on TV when the hero peels out. Plus peeling out is something else our Caravan isn't too good at.

But I barely noticed because all I could think about was that expression on Brian's face. What *was* that? I didn't get it. It was like that time in Taco Bell, only worse because this time his friends weren't even being jerks. Not that they were jerks in Taco Bell, but they could have been—I mean, if they'd seen me, and seen the other Red Bend players. And they sure were jerks last summer, calling me names right to my face. And roughing me up during the scrimmage.

It made me feel sick inside. If Brian was, you know, sleeping with me or something and then blowing me off in front of his friends, that I could understand. That happens all the time, boys using girls like that. But his behavior just now I didn't understand at all. All those long talks we'd had these past weeks as he'd told me how great I was, listening to my depressing life. All those times he came to the farm super early on weekend mornings when he could have been asleep, the meals he had with us and all the help he provided without even being asked. And all that kissing too, which he didn't have to do but that, duh, he really seemed to enjoy . . . Call me crazy, but isn't that the stuff you do when you like a girl? Like her for her company and her family, and her feelings? Whenever the two of us were together, we had a special connection. I felt it, and I know he felt it too. He *did* like me. He liked me a lot. Which meant his expression now wasn't just blowing off some dumb girl you really don't care about. It meant he was embarrassed about me.

I was almost home before I remembered Curtis and had to turn around. He wasn't very happy to see me, especially with Sarah's mom so pleased with him again, but he caught sight of my face and drove with me to the truck right away, not saying a word, which was good because if he had, I would have removed his head right from his body and put it in a box for the next middle school science fair.

It was pitch dark when we walked into the house finally, Smut so relieved because it was way past her dinner, which I'd forgotten about. Curtis hit the answering machine button that was blinking away although I didn't care one bit, and the very first message, from nine o'clock that morning, was Dad.

"D.J.? Pick up, sport. Your mother, she hurt her back again, really bad . . . We need you here. We need you to stay."

And all the rest of the messages said the same thing only with curse words by the end because Dad couldn't figure out where I was, and why I wouldn't answer my cell phone either.

It's not like I'd been ignoring Dad on purpose, you know, I'd just forgotten to take my cell. Which I got him to admit after about ten minutes of cussing me out, that maybe it was an honest mistake. Then Kathy Ott showed up—she'd been talking to Dad all day and sounded just as stressed as he was—and said she'd spend the night with Curtis so I could drive back to the hospital as soon as possible.

I suppose I could have said I wouldn't do it. That's what some people would say and they have a right to, I guess, when the situation gets too overwhelming. I sure didn't want to go back to Minnesota and Win, no matter how much Mom needed me. But I couldn't come up with any other solutions; I needed a couple days just to figure out what had happened with Brian. It's not like I decided that thinking about Brian would be a great thing to do in Minnesota, though. It's more that I wasn't thinking, period. Instead I stuffed a bunch of stuff in a duffel, more stuff this time because who knew how long I'd be there, and a basketball in case I had some free time to practice, although at the moment the chances of me playing girls' basketball were looking about as probable as me playing for the Vikings.

I said goodbye to Kathy and Smut, who'd gotten fed at least, and to Curtis. Dad called again and Kathy said, "She just left," and told me to drive safe because Mom wasn't there to say it, and off I went.

At least my cell phone was charged. And I had a ton of messages, which I didn't want to check one bit but I needed to erase them, and most were from Dad still cussing me out, and then a happy-sounding one from Amber checking in, and the last one was from Brian.

"I'm so sorry about what just happened. I really screwed up. Please call me."

I erased that one too. It's not like keeping it would help any. And I didn't call him back. I wasn't ready for that yet.

Instead I drove our rattling Caravan on the same highway Jimmy took to drive Dad and me to the airport, and that Brian used for the Mall of America. That Mall of America trip had been one of the best days of my life. And not just because we ended up making out like movie stars at the rest area I was just passing now, the Brian Nelson Memorial Make-Out Truck Stop. It was because that whole day he'd been so great. He bragged about my football to everyone and he kept really close to me with hundreds of people all around us, he even put his arm around my shoulders when we were looking at something extra exciting. Plus he got me that cell phone, and even paid for my pierced ears.

But — I suddenly realized with a gasp — you know why? To make me cooler. I could see it now. I mean, the earrings looked good although by this point I didn't even notice them. And calling our house on the home phone probably wasn't much fun. But that day he wanted to buy me so much more, and get me to buy more, clothes that were cool even though I didn't need them, and CDs of music I don't care about. And it was only after coming back from the mall with my brand-new earrings that he kissed me. Because by that point I guess I was cool enough.

But not *really* cool enough, or he wouldn't totally ignore me whenever we ran into each other, and refuse to invite me out with his friends or go with me to the movies, and then uninvite me — or try to if I hadn't uninvited myself already — that one Saturday we were planning to watch TV at his house, once it looked like his friends were coming over. Because apparently blowing me off was easier than disappointing them. Because being my kind-of boyfriend in the Mall of America with thousands of strangers, or with that tailgate guy, or those two turkey farmer reporters didn't bother him one little teeny atom as much as it bothered him to be seen with me in Taco Bell in front of his buddies.

Maybe that was the solution to all this. If I could find a

place, if Brian and I could find a place where no one knew us, then we could do whatever we wanted and be happy about it. A town full of strangers.

As soon as this thought came into my head, though, I knew it wouldn't work. Someone would always know one of us. That's why Brian had gotten so upset about *People*. I mean, I got upset too, I'm not denying that, and I sure took a lot of grief about it. It's not like I wanted the entire United States to know about the two of us. But at least I wasn't *embarrassed* about him.

Just then my cell phone rang: Brian.

Wait a minute, I said to my paranoid and miserable brain. Brian isn't like that. There must be another explanation of all this, and he had a right to explain it. If he was brave enough to call me — to call me twice — then I could talk to him at least.

"Hey," I answered.

"Jeez, I'm glad you picked up."

Just hearing his voice made me feel so much better. Almost all better, in fact. Just those few words. "No problem," I said. "So, how's it going?"

"I called your house looking for you, and Curtis said you were going back to Minnesota. Is everything okay?"

"Mom's back went out again . . . Listen, I never, you know, asked you, but remember that *People* magazine thing?"

Brian laughed. "Yeah. Why, are they doing a sequel?"

"No. Um, wait—would that be a bad thing?"

"Are you kidding? Just tell me now so I can leave town."
He chuckled again.

"It was that bad, huh?"

"You have no idea. The crap I got, you don't even want to know."

"Because I was from Red Bend?"

He paused. "Yeah. My friends had no idea I was, you know, seeing you. They—they don't know what someone like you is like."

"What do you mean, someone like me?"

"Well, you know . . . You're really different."

"Meaning I'm not cool." And it was kind of icy, the way this came out.

"Come on, you know how kids are. I'm sure your friends acted the same way."

"Actually, my *friends* didn't. They thought it was okay. They even thought you were cute. And they're *lesbians*." Which was the first time I ever said that word out loud, and I hope it never gets back to Amber and Dale, my using them like that. Although it sure felt good at the moment.

"Oh," said Brian. Because that was a curve ball, I admit.

"Is it uncool when we make out? Is it uncool when we talk about Win and all his problems?"

"D.J.! You think I don't feel bad about what happened tonight? You didn't even warn me you were coming by!"

"Yeah, it's my fault I don't *warn* you whenever I appear in public."

"That wasn't public—don't do this. We have a complicated relationship, okay? It's not normal."

"I'm not normal?"

"That's not what I said! And by the way, you're not. Normal means average. Average girls aren't six feet tall, and they don't play football or run dairy farms, and they date . . ."

"Who do they date?" I needed to hear this, what he said.

Brian sighed. "I did not want to be attracted to you. Don't you understand? It was not something I did on purpose, it was something I fought. Because I knew how hard it would be."

"More than hard, it sounds like," I said. "I guess I'm just too big for you."

"Jeez, D.J. I feel so bad right now—"

"Yeah, well, go tell your friends." Then I hung up.

All this time I'd thought Brian was brave because he could talk about really painful subjects. Like just now when he said how bad he felt—that's something Schwenks suck at, discussing feelings. I'd thought how great he was too. But a guy who's really great would have friends who are great as well. Not friends who make fun of me and badmouth me all the time. And if friends did do that, a guy who was really brave would be able to make them stop. And invite me over to his house, and to the movies, and say hello when he saw me on the street even if that street was Hawley High School.

Brian wasn't brave. Talk is easy, compared to action. Brian was a coward. And worse than that, he wasn't my friend. This whole time he'd been using me, like a guy uses a girl for fooling around but in a different way. A worse way, even. He was pretending we were really close, that we were girlfriend and boyfriend even, but only on our farm and at the Mall of America where it didn't matter. Where he wouldn't upset his real friends. And that's why finding a town full of strangers to live in wouldn't work out ever. Because he'd always be looking over his shoulder to make sure he wasn't going to get caught with his embarrassing pretend pal, D.J.

22

REHAB

DAD AND BILL WERE INTO THEIR FIFTH BEERS, it looked like, when I got to the apartment, and Mom was asleep on the floor with a couple pill bottles beside her. I popped myself a beer, which is pretty unusual for me but what the hey, and slumped at the table next to Dad. Bill was turning the beer can in his hand like he'd been doing it for hours without even noticing. Dad didn't react to any of this. He just sat there, looking so much like Grandpa Warren. So old. "Jesus. What are we gonna do?" he sighed.

Which sort of put a damper in my plans to announce that Brian and I had broken up. It's not like I much wanted to say it anyway, seeing as I'd never even really discussed the fact we were going out, but I'd figured I could at least be brave enough to speak the words. Now, though, I didn't think another dose of bad news would be too helpful. So instead we sat together and finished our beers without saying anything, which I think is the conversation we needed most.

Bill and I saw Mom and Dad off the next morning, helping Mom into the back of the Caravan and me telling her over and over again—lying over and over again—that it was absolutely okay for her to be going home, and that I really wanted to be here, and that she needed to heal so that she could help Win later. Between all the stress of Win's injury plus trying to lift him, she'd brought the slipped disk right back, and now she was at square one again. She was pretty doped up on pain pills, which was good because that ride home was going to be a monster, but still she tried to give me all these instructions on taking care of Win, to keep telling him we loved him. Her clothes hung on her so much that I was afraid her pants were going to slip right off, and then I realized it was because she'd lost so much weight.

"Keep feeding her, Dad," I said as they left, which is something I never thought I'd say to my father. I didn't bother asking how long I'd be staying because I had a feeling it was going to be something like "As long as it takes," only no one knew what "it" was and no one wanted to talk about it. Then I waved at them, faking a smile, and watched them drive away. Just like Dale and Amber had driven off, only they were going in the opposite direction. And I walked into the hospital next to Bill, who was so hunched over that he looked as shriveled as Mom. He didn't even get checked out by the nurses, that's how bad it was. They just looked bummed out too.

The next couple days, oh boy. Win wasn't cooperating at all. He wouldn't even answer the PTs when they asked if he felt dizzy. One big thing with SCI is blood pressure, and when patients first sit up—which makes anyone dizzy if you do it too fast, even regular people—they have to be really careful. They might only sit up halfway, or one fifth, even, until everything gets stabilized a bit. It might take a couple days of practice just to get all the way up.

The PTs said that as soon as he could sit up, we'd all get to practice moving him into a wheelchair so he could go down to the cafeteria to eat. They're really caught up in having everyone eat together so patients can get to know one another, and staff too, and families. I couldn't help but think that hell would freeze over solid before Win sat at a table chatting it up, and then once I saw the cafeteria, I got even more worried.

The room itself was really nice, with photos on the walls of all sorts of patients who were now Successful at Life. And it had the counters of food and trays and stuff just like any cafeteria space. Only all the shelves and doors were built with wheelchairs in mind, and the tables had very few chairs because, duh, most of the people arrived with their own. Some of the tables were extra high for the patients in power wheelchairs because those seats are higher than normal, and the regular walking people sat at those tables like they were kindergarten-size or something, the table up around their armpits. The silverware holders had forks and spoons with extra-long handles so patients whose hands didn't work so well could still feed themselves, and a lot of the plates and bowls had suction cup bottoms so those patients wouldn't knock them off their trays as they ate. Some of the patients were eating with spoons strapped to their arms, and others who couldn't move at all, the complete quads, were being spoon-fed by aides or by their family members sometimes, their caregivers.

All of a sudden I almost lost it, realizing this was Win's future, and I had to drop my head down and squeeze my eyes shut tight, and hope with all my heart that my tears wouldn't ooze through anyway and drop with a splat on the floor.

"It's really hard, coming here for the first time," said Maryann, the PT who was showing me around. "Some people just fall apart." She waited a minute, then she added, "They've got some really good vegetarian chili today. Are you a vegetarian?"

Now, I don't know if she asked that because she was sincerely curious or because she was just trying to change the subject—which shows how nice she is—but even in all my misery I couldn't help but snort because the thought of me being a vegetarian is right up there with the thought of me becoming president of the United States. "Do they have any real food?" I asked. And then remembering my manners I added, "I mean, not that there's anything wrong with being a vegetarian. I mean, it's okay to be one—if, you know, you are already."

She laughed. "Only with chili."

After we got our food, she sat with me at a table with an L3. I was really glad that he was lumbar and not cervical because if I'd had to watch him struggle away with one of those spoon tools, I would have lost it for real. He and Maryann didn't talk to me too much — I guess they could tell I was on the far side of fragile — they just chatted about PT and wheelchairs, this new model he was thinking of getting, while I worked through my vegetarian chili and tried my hardest not to cry.

Bill and I would sit with Win, hours passing without us saying a word, or Bill would spell me. I took mornings and nights, and he was there in the middle of the day because he's stronger and could help more with the transferring. So I'd have long, long stretches pretty much alone, with so many thoughts inside my head that I worried sometimes my skull would just explode right off my neck, like a balloon pumped with too much air. Especially when I thought about Brian.

I couldn't believe that Brian and I were . . . I didn't know what we were, actually. It was more than a breakup, because our friendship was over as well. Our so-called friendship. I didn't want to be friends with him, not for a long while anyway. Because even if he promised he'd change, and promised to defend me to all his friends or take me to the movies or whatever, I wouldn't trust him. Because being embarrassed about someone isn't something you can change, any more than you can change being spooked about needles. Only it was a lot harder to be sympathetic about Brian than it was Dad.

I guess you could say my feelings were hurt.

And Brian didn't call again. I don't know if that makes him brave or wimpy—I still haven't figured that one out—but I was glad. Well, actually I was horribly miserable and spent hours on end wishing I could talk to him. But it was better that he didn't call. No matter what my brain was wishing, I still needed time to figure this stuff out.

Plus now that I was stuck in Minnesota taking care of Win, my life—the life I'd just left behind in Red Bend, for who knows how long—didn't look so bad, even without Brian being part of it. If I was at home, I could be going to school and actually getting help with all my assignments instead of being stuck with a huge pile of books and head-scratching homework that Mom had asked all the teachers to send me, each of them giving me their home phone number like the one thing I wanted to do most in the world was call my Spanish teacher about all the vocabulary words I'd missed, or my world history teacher about China. Every night I'd bring a pile of books and papers to the hospital and sit there straining my brain over math or whatever, sometimes with Win facing me if he'd been rolled on his side, a pillow between his knees to prevent bedsores, but he never once asked me to lob him some algebra problems just to pass the time.

If I was at home, though, maybe Curtis could help me with algebra, he's so smart, and I could cheer him up about the science fair, help him be less intimidated by the kind of kids who wouldn't know a science fair if it bit them on the butt.

If I was at home, I could be getting ready for basketball. That time I'd spent shooting baskets in our driveway, right before Curtis had ended my big forty-five minute day of rest, had been quite a wake-up call, actually. Kind of like when I decided to play football last summer only I've played b-ball my whole life. If I were on the team, scouts would see me, and maybe I'd end up with a scholarship and that college degree everyone thinks is so important. But now, though, that was impossible. No high school, no basketball season, no scholarship, no college, no future.

And I'd think about Amber, who was in St. Paul right now working with Dale. She kept asking how she could help but she couldn't do a darn thing. Heck, she couldn't even help out with Mom's slipped disk because she'd run away from Red Bend just because her moron mother got mad at her and some kids at school said things that someone as tough as Amber should be able to handle. But no, she took the easy route and split, her so-called grown-up girlfriend not even stopping her because all *she* worried about were stupid things like jobs and diplomas, when they both could have worried for maybe two seconds about, well, about me.

Then Amber called to say they were moving to Chicago, and could they stop by to say goodbye.

23

WHY THE PACKERS MIGHT NOT
TOTALLY SUCK

THE THREE OF US went for lunch in the hospital cafeteria. I'd asked Bill if he wanted to come down—hoping he wouldn't but you still have to ask. He said no. I guess seeing other people's friends would have been too depressing, not to mention the cafeteria itself.

I was pretty used to it by now seeing as I ate at least one meal a day there, even if it was only sandwiches I'd made in our little apartment, or a bowl of cereal. Dale and Amber were pretty blown away by it, though. The place was full of all sorts of wheelchair folks, from the man on the ventilator being spoon-fed by his wife, it looked like, to a couple of muscle guys in pro jerseys who looked like they'd just come off the basketball court, one of them even with a b-ball in a special bag on the back of his chair.

Amber and Dale's eyes got awfully wide, taking it in. Dale looked at me with so much honest concern that tears started prickling my head.

"So . . . you in school yet?" I asked Amber.

Which got Amber going because she was even less interested in my crying than I was, which I appreciated, describing this beauty school in Chicago she hoped to get into, which led to a couple funny stories about her hair disasters, most of them on me, that got us all laughing, and got my mind for one minute off our family's problems.

"How's that man of yours?" Dale asked, grinning at me.

I shrugged. "We — I don't know — we broke up."

Amber tried to look sympathetic.

"That stinks," Dale sighed. "He seemed like a nice guy."

"Yeah, he was. He still is, I'm sure."

"Not much of a boat rocker though, is he?" And from the way Dale smiled at me, I knew she understood everything that had happened.

"Yeah, but he was pretty cute," Amber said. Which was nice, her endorsing Brian like that.

It felt so good to be having this conversation, just like when we were all sitting in Dale's camper outside McDonald's. Girl talk. Which I wouldn't be able to have ever again, now that they were taking off.

All of a sudden, these words popped out of my mouth: "Please don't go. Come back to Red Bend. I need you there."

"Well, I can't." Amber scowled down at her tray. "And you know why."

"You can't control what people say about you, you know," Dale said. Which kind of drove home that she wasn't all that unfamiliar with people's stares and nasty whispers.

Amber gathered up her tray. "But I can blow them off. Come on, we got a lot of driving to do."

I walked them out to the camper. I thought about tossing out a Bob the duck line, something like, "Hey baby, can you take me south with you?" But it would have been far too depressing, on every level I could think of. Instead I just waved goodbye to them, and almost started bawling as they drove away from everything I couldn't leave, and from the most honest and heartfelt request I've ever made of Amber. If I ever made it back to Red Bend, it would suck ten times more with them gone. Even if Amber didn't play basketball, it still would have been nice to have her around. And maybe I could have talked her into playing somehow, the team really needed her . . .

I know I sound pretty selfish — not just my complaining, but also that I'm not really describing Win and what he was going through, which was a heck of a lot more than I was. But you know, there wasn't much to say. He wasn't improving, he was barely talking, and he still wasn't interested in telling the doctors or Bill or me what sort of pinpricks or dizziness he could feel, or in trying to move, or in talking to the psychia-lady — only here it was a psychia-man — about his emotions, or in anything. He just lay there staring at the ceiling, or at the wall if he was rolled that way. And late at night he cried. Which I still helped him with, that one little bit I could do.

Going back up to the room, I remembered one time that Win got punished for something, probably not doing a job exactly how Dad wanted, and when Mom sat down next to him on the couch, he turned his back on her. And she said — because she's a mom and not a normal person who'd call him a jerk — she said he was trying to push her away but she wouldn't let him. And in the end, because she's a mom, he didn't.

Win was doing the same thing now, trying to push us away so he could be miserable all by himself. And I guess it worked with Mom, at least in the sense that her back went out so she couldn't hang around telling him she loved him. And guess what? It was going to work with me too. Because if Win was that unhappy, that absolutely miserable, well, I wasn't sure anyone could change him.

When I got up to our floor, a guy in a Packers jacket was in the hall talking to Bill. Which is odd because this is Minnesota — Vikings country — and a Green Bay fan walking around like that is just inviting attention. Which is why I don't wear my Vikings jersey in Red Bend except with my Vikings-fans family, and pretty much the only good thing about this hospital was that I now could wear that jersey in public.

The Packers guy, though, looked like he didn't care that most people on the floor would cheer if his team lost. He was a big guy, with a gut like old football players get, and he kept looking at Win's door and nodding as he and Bill talked.

Bill waved me over, looking happier than I'd seen him in weeks, and tossed one of his big arms around my shoulders to introduce me. "This is our sister, D.J."

The guy shook my hand and said he was an old friend of Charlie Wright's, and an offensive coordinator with the Packers.

"Oh," I said. I'd never shaken hands with a pro coach before.

"You let your brother know we're serious, okay? Charlie can't say enough about him, and us getting a go-getter like that—I know he'd be a real asset."

"What—you . . . you offered him a *job?*"

"It's just an assistant's position with the conditioning team. But we'd sure like to have him." The guy handed a card to Bill. "That's my cell number on the back. We're in town for the weekend."

"But—" I said the first, stupidest thing that came to mind. "But we're Vikings fans."

Bill cracked up. The guy too. "There are worse crimes," he said. "Enjoy the game tomorrow." He grinned at us as he got on the elevator.

Bill stood there holding that card like it was a baby. "Well, shoot. What do you think of that?"

"What's Win say about it?" I asked.

"Dunno. I came back from talking to Mom and that guy was just walking out."

So the two of us scooted over to Win's room, knowing already this would make the difference.

Only it didn't.

"Get out!" Win snarled as soon as he heard us. He could barely talk, he was so angry. Tears ran down his face. "Disappear! I don't want to see you! Don't you get it?"

"That guy just offered you a job," Bill said.

"Yeah, right. A 'job' being the cripple in the wheelchair — 'Oh, isn't he brave, look how good football is to him.' It's complete crap."

"It didn't sound like that to me," I put in.

"You're not the one lying here. So why don't both of you just get out of my room. And while you're at it, go home! I don't need your pity, I don't need your help, I don't need anyone." He lay there glaring at us, the collar looking almost like football gear around his neck, and for a moment I thought he was going to climb right out of that bed and start swinging, he seemed so full of anger. So full of life.

And, well, I snapped. All the garbage I'd been through, all the stress of Brian and Amber and Curtis and Dad and my shoulder and Mom's back and our lack of money, not to mention all the stress of Win, all of a sudden exploded right out of me. And that's when it happened.

24

THERE AREN'T NO MIRACLES ON SCHWENK FARM

GRANDPA WARREN WAS ABOUT the most nonreligious person I know. He wasn't one of those atheists always complaining about nativity scenes and stuff—those folks are just as pushy as some born-agains. It's more that he didn't care. He only went to church that one time, and while he might mention God in cussing, mostly the higher powers stayed out of his conversation altogether. I asked him once if he believed in heaven, and he said he was a farmer, he was happy just being dirt.

One summer he cleaned out our raggedy old toolshed, which is a huge project, getting all covered with grease and rust and cobwebs, taking a couple beers with him in the afternoons to ease the pain. Well, after a full week including Sunday he got it done, and of course we all went to see because we were curious and also it would have set him off if we hadn't, and we stood there gaping at all those perfect shelves, the tools where they should be for once, the lawn tractor with all its attachments hanging like a store display or something.

"Why, Warren, it's a miracle in here," said Mom.

Grandpa Warren snorted. "There aren't no miracles on Schwenk Farm, Linda. You know that." Then he went on to say that if God had been out there cleaning the shed, He sure had kept His presence quiet, and that next time Grandpa would appreciate a little more participation on the Lord's part, should He be so inclined.

I've thought about this story a lot these past weeks. Of course Win is named after Grandpa and all, but mainly I can't help thinking about it whenever anyone uses that word "miracle." Every time I hear it I nod, or shrug if I'm in that kind of mood, and think that I could have used more of the Lord's participation in those first weeks, and in the weeks following to tell you the truth. I'll probably end up getting hit by a thunderbolt or something, but I can't help it.

And if I don't get hit by a thunderbolt for being sacrilegious, I'll get hit for being just plain mean because that's what I was. I won't lie.

Because what happened was, I stood there glaring at Win lying there so furious, unable even to wipe his eyes and yet still looking like he could jump right up, and I blasted him.

"You have *no* idea, do you? You have no idea who you are. All you can think about is how *sorry* everyone feels for you, how you want to *die.* Fine, go ahead. The Packers will find someone else. There are two thousand guys out there who'd cut their arm off to work for that team. Guys who know everything there is to know about football. Some of them maybe even know more than you. Do you think? Do you think that maybe out there in this entire enormous country is one person who knows more about football than you do?" Oh, I was hot.

Bill gaped at me. At least I think he did. I was too mad to really notice.

"Shut up," Win snarled.

"Yeah, probably. But none of them are getting offered jobs. Not because they're not *crippled*. Not because their necks aren't broken. It's because they're not you. They want *you*."

"Shut *up!*"

"You—in high school you got twenty guys to come out all summer to a field full of cow poop, their moms driving them at six in the morning sometimes, because of *you*. Because you care so much you get everyone else caring too. And that doesn't have anything to do with your neck or your body. It's just who you are."

I was crying now, I admit. I could barely talk, I was crying so hard. Bill had backed himself into the corner trying to get away—he'd have climbed out the window if he could, probably.

"I swear to God, Win, you could crawl across the grass with your teeth and you'd still make those players care. You could coach anything—you could coach basketball. You could coach me! And if you throw away a chance at pro ball when most guys work twenty years for one shot—when Bill's giving up his whole life, and me too, just to take care of you . . . Fine. As far as I'm concerned, my brother is already dead."

Which was kind of a dramatic exit line for someone who usually thinks them up three or four weeks later. But I stomped right out because if I hadn't, I would have punched him. And I raced into the bathroom with the wide doors and the special low sinks and tilted mirrors and locked myself in the handicapped stall because right then I didn't care about any handicapped female who might need to pee, and I cried. I sat in the corner, my head against that cold tile wall, and I sobbed. I couldn't go on like this. I really couldn't. Dr. Rosenberger had said that people who want to die usually succeed, and right now that was looking like a pretty good option for me. I could jump off the building maybe, although that would require leaving the bathroom. Or take some of those pills that people on TV always seem to have available when they want to off themselves, if only I knew what kinds of pills those were. And had some.

It was pretty comfortable sitting here, actually—a lot more comfortable than the bathroom at home. It didn't smell. Probably got cleaned every day. I could stay here awhile, which wouldn't be a bad thing seeing as I was beginning to wonder how loud I'd been, how much the nurses had heard me bawling out my crippled brother. Which I'm pretty sure you're not supposed to do no matter how much they deserve it. Those nurses were probably calling a psychia-lady right now, getting ready to take me away.

Someone came into the bathroom, and I pulled my feet in close so I wouldn't get seen. The footsteps got closer until they were right outside my door.

"D.J.?"

It was Bill. He peered over the top of the stall. "Could you come out here a minute?"

"You're not supposed to be in here, you know," I managed to say. Then with a big sigh I stood up and tried to get past him without showing my face and all its red tear marks, and washed some of them off while he waited, and he handed me a paper towel, which was nice, and walked me back to Win's room.

"Do it again," a nurse was saying with this really strange expression, her eyes on Win's right foot.

And Win, with a look of total concentration, wiggled his toes.

I screamed. I didn't even realize I was screaming until Bill threw his arms around me and spun me in the air like I weighed absolutely nothing, which I don't, and the nurse grabbed the phone to page the doctor because nothing counts until a doctor sees it.

"Jeez, you two, chill out," Win said.

And the doctor came and Win did it again, and then tried

to do his other foot and almost could, you could see the muscles flexing sometimes, which is what really matters, and then he said he was really tired and wanted to sleep. So the doctor left to go write this all up, and Bill and I rearranged Win like you should, and he closed his eyes.

"Sweet dreams, bro," Bill said. Bill looked fit to burst, he was so happy.

I adjusted his sheets, bursting myself, just itching to call Mom and tell her.

"Hey, D.J.," Win whispered. "Wear your b-ball shoes tomorrow."

"What?" I asked. "What are you talking about?"

He shut his eyes, already half asleep. "Because I'm your new coach."

Mom called it a miracle, of course. But like I said, it's not. I don't think it is, anyway. Bill and I have talked a lot about it, and you know what I think? Those first weeks that Win couldn't move his body or feel anything, he was still too caught up in football and not being able to play. He wouldn't let himself feel—literally—anything else. Win even told me later—he was kind of sheepish about it, to his credit—that he'd had a hunch for a while that he could wiggle his toes a bit. He'd practice sometimes when he was alone. But he didn't tell anyone because he wasn't talking for one thing, and also because he was afraid it might not be true, and that even if it was true, he wouldn't be able to do it when people asked, because if you can't move "at will," it doesn't count. Also I think he didn't tell anyone because to his mind wiggling his toes was so insignificant compared to what he used to be able to do, especially when even trying to wiggle took every bit of his concentration. And it wasn't until he'd been presented with some real options, coaching options, that he began to see that toe wiggling might actually lead to something worthwhile.

I mean, I'm not a psychia-lady or anything but that's my theory, and Bill at least thinks it's a pretty good one, not that he's got any more brains than I do for this stuff. Also, I have a suspicion it was getting a little boring even for Win just to lie there all day feeling sorry for himself and yelling at people. As boring as it was getting for everyone else.

And let me clarify: it wasn't like, Win is cured! That little toe movement was the first tiny step of a huge trip. So don't think it ended, all the work and the huge fights, the crying and screaming sometimes. In a lot of ways, that story is just beginning.

Which brings up *another* story that's kind of relevant to this whole thing. Remember Win and his baseball cards, how he didn't talk to Bill for a month? Well, I forgot to mention — because I forgot myself, forgot until after I'd yelled at him — how it ended. We were all at dinner, Win totally ignoring Bill like he'd been doing for weeks, and Dad turned to Win and said, "This isn't how a captain acts, you know."

Win got up and stomped into the bathroom. I remember

whispering, "Uh-oh" to myself, because even then Win could, you know, determine the mood of a room. After a couple minutes the toilet flushed and Win came out wiping his hands on his shirt, and he sat down and said to Bill, "Pass the potatoes, could you?" And that was the end of that. Like absolutely nothing had happened.

Sound kind of familiar?

25

WIN WASN'T CAPTAIN FOR NOTHING

To TELL YOU THE TRUTH, there were times I really missed Win sulking because it wasn't such a barrel of monkeys now that he was talking again. I don't know how a patient is supposed to act, but I have a feeling that bugging the doctors with a million questions, and demanding *real* rehab right in the middle of physical therapy, and getting on my case a hundred times a day about basketball—and all of this on major painkillers and muscle relaxants and stuff . . . I mean, that's a lot.

Plus he told Bill to go back to college. Ordered him, really. He said Bill needed to keep playing football no matter what because his team needed him and so did the pros, and it was just a horribly bad and wimpy idea for Bill to even *think* about dropping football—which Bill had talked about with me a couple times as the two of us sat next to Win's bed back when he ignored us and pretended to be asleep. Which showed now just how much he'd been faking, because he lit into Bill about how rare injuries like his were, and how Bill needed to show courage for the other players, and for Win too. It was like a movie speech or something.

Plus he said it was a waste of time for Bill to hang around the hospital when Win had me. Which I think he meant as a compliment, that I was so helpful and stuff. So Bill made us promise to call every day and send pictures, and keep some beer in the fridge for him, and he gave me a huge hug and started crying, saying I'd saved Win's life, which was a little heavy, and then I got stuck with the SCI Energizer Bunny.

I've always said Win was born to be a coach — just look at that big inspiring speech he gave Bill. Well, once Bill listened to him and left, Win didn't have anyone else to take his coaching urges out on, the way some dogs need to chew and will use a shoe if they don't have a stick or a bone to work on. So he took them out on me.

The first thing he did was grill me on my shoulder, and insisted the rehab doctors look at it. They said, maybe just to shut him up, that I should take it easy throwing still and do all those PT exercises I'd let slide, and Win looked at me like, Hey, your problems are over. Then he pointed out I was looking pretty flabby there. Weeks of sitting around the hospital, plus resting my shoulder and taking care of Mom, hadn't done anything for my strength, or my wind, which he said like it was my fault and wouldn't even admit that he might have had something to do with it, and instead he just told me to wear workout clothes when I came in every day. Just so you know, this was one of those times I wished he'd go back to sulking. But I kept that to myself.

Because he was now *recovering* and all, Win was totally

into a bunch of stuff he'd flat-out rejected a few days before, like traveling around the hospital in a wheelchair. Which was a huge bunch of PT in and of itself, learning to transfer from the bed to the chair with a PT helping him, and her teaching the two of us how to do it ourselves. The first big trip we took off the floor, we visited the hospital gym, and it just about broke my heart. A couple guys in those loose pants paras wear when they're first practicing how to dress themselves sat there struggling to shoot from their chairs, every basket — every throw — taking so much effort. That was one of the bad times, actually, when Win went back to his old self for a while, not talking at all or helping me transfer him to bed. It wasn't until he slept for a couple hours, and cried some from the looks of it, that he returned to being bossy and extra hard-working.

Luckily, pretty soon after Win's change of heart and Bill's departure, I was in his room reading him this article and trying to decipher the medical mumbo jumbo with a big textbook from the rehab library when this guy wheeled in. He wasn't the kind of individual you see much of in Red Bend, and I don't just mean the wheelchair. He was shaved bald with tattoos up and down his arms, and fingerless gloves and huge basketball sneakers that looked like they'd never been used. Which, duh, they hadn't.

"And how are you two doing today?" he asked. Like he was a salesman or something.

"Okay," I said, kind of cautiously.

If he took offense, though, he didn't show it. "I am Dennis, the one-man committee of welcome. I know all about you," he said to Win. "You're a football C5 incomplete. But I don't know you," he added, pointing at me.

"I'm, um, his sister. D.J."

"Well, little sister, come sit in my lap." He patted his bony legs, then laughed at my face. "Don't worry! You should see the size of some of the ladies I've had here." He grinned at Win.

I was shocked—completely and totally shocked. But Win just grinned back. "That a fact?"

"This chair is like honey to a bee. Girls come around like, 'Oh, aren't you something.'" All of a sudden Dennis grabbed his wheels and—boom!—tipped over on his back, so far his head almost touched the floor. Like he was having a seizure or something. I gave this huge holler and Win gasped, and all at once Dennis was sitting right back up again—he'd pulled himself up.

Well, that knocked us out.

Dennis grinned. "You see that? That's a thunderball trick I know."

"What's thunderball?" Win asked.

"It's basketball for *men*. Basketball for wheelers. You play any hoops?"

"A bit, in high school."

"Well, you need to get out there, get yourself some

moves." He wheeled closer to the bed. "Listen, don't you go badmouthing the chair. Everyone's hung up on walking like it's a trophy or something. Well, you can spend the rest of your life trying to walk or you can spend the rest of your life living. You hear what I'm saying?" He made a fist and reached out to Win.

Win couldn't make a fist, but he raised his arm enough to connect.

"You two come on down to the gym, you'll see some real ball." He rolled out, popping a wheelie.

I blinked after him. "Jeez."

Win didn't say anything. But he stared at the doorway for some time.

The next time Win and I stopped by the gym, Dennis and some other guys in big elbow pads were playing pickup, and after a couple seconds it was clear that shooting was the least of their problems—the main issue was that one of them was going to get killed. They'd crash into each other, and wave their arms in each other's faces just like real b-ball players only they were spinning their wheelchairs everywhere, and their language wasn't something you'd want your grandma hearing.

"Hey there!" Dennis came zooming over. "How are ya?"

"You got an extra ball?" Win asked.

"Sure thing. You ready to give it a try?"

"Not me," Win said, rolling his eyes in my direction.

Dennis looked me over. "I see what you mean there . . ."

At first I thought Win was going to make me play pickup with them, which I wouldn't do no matter what — it wasn't fair because I could intercept just about any shot, and it also wasn't fair because they'd roll into me and I'd end up with a broken leg. Instead I went to the other end of the court and started shooting three-pointers, keeping it gentle to hold off that shoulder twinge.

"Oooh," I could hear Dennis behind me. "Check it out there!"

"Drop the camera," Win said from the sidelines, which I learned was his term for showing off. "You're playing! Make a space for yourself." Which meant don't just shoot, but use my elbows like I had two defenders on me, and spin a little, and dribble, and imagine the game and the pressure instead of just playing Horse.

Win seemed to feel I was just about the worst basketball player he'd ever seen. He kept yelling all the things I should be doing. Plus he was turning his whole body as much as possible, using all the muscles he could, to watch my shots because of course he couldn't turn his head. Within fifteen minutes we were both soaked, and he was so hoarse he could barely talk. But he talked enough to order some wind sprints, which I did even though I didn't want to because, well, he's Win, and also I knew sure as shooting that wind sprints happen every day at b-ball and I might as well get used to them.

I was pretty embarrassed to be running in front of Dennis and his friends, but Dennis came right out and rolled beside me, chattering the whole time, and it was all I could do to stay ahead of him because my shoes are so old that they don't have much grip left but it's not like I had a big wad of money available to buy new ones. That wouldn't count as a Mom's-credit-card emergency no matter how much Dennis busted me for being slow.

When we got back upstairs, Win just drooped, he was so exhausted. But he still told me all the drills we'd do tomorrow.

Only the gym was so crowded most times that I couldn't do much, and other times I just plain refused because watching a girl with two good legs wasn't something the guys in there needed at that specific moment. Once Win got on my case so much that I had to remind him of his first time there, and then at least he had the grace to shut up.

Instead he found out the gym didn't open until seven, and he asked around some more and got a gym key, which was kind of funny seeing as his hands didn't work so well—and whenever he tried to do anything it looked like he was wearing giant oven mitts. The very act of picking up a key was half an hour of PT right there. Which should make you count your blessings, thinking about that.

And which explains why the hospital folks let us do it at all. We were down there at six-thirty one morning—Win "let" me come in at five to get him up so we could be in the gym by five-thirty for a good ninety-minute workout before the PTs took it over—and I was practicing foul shots. Whenever I made one, the ball would land pretty close to Win and sometimes he could get a hand out enough to slow it down and nudge it back my way.

Just then, one of Win's doctors walked in. He stood for about ten minutes watching, although I was so mad I really didn't think about it much. Win had gotten himself a whistle—Maryann gave it to him, actually, the PT who was so nice to me that first week, and it was a huge deal for him just to get the whistle into his mouth because he was just getting his pinch and grasp movements back. It took a couple minutes each time and he'd finally get it in there, but then he'd come up with something he *had* to tell me and spit the whistle out, only to struggle away to put it back in and then to blow it. Even though we were the only people in the gym! It wasn't like he had to get my attention, make sure I could hear him over the noise—I could hear him just fine. And so every time he blew that thing, I got a little bit angrier, and every time he'd spit it out to tell me something I already knew, I'd get a little more, and I was about ready to rip that whistle right off its cord. Which is probably a good thing for Win, then, that the doctor showed up.

So the doctor kept watching, especially how Win was using his hands to roll himself to the closer basketballs, which is really technical because the wheelchair has to end up exactly the right distance from the ball, especially when you're strapped in and wearing a cervical collar and thick rubber-surfaced gloves so you can get your second-rate hands to move the chair at all.

"Are we doing anything wrong?" I asked finally, just in case there was something about how Win was moving, or even our just being there, that we should know.

"You're providing the best therapy in the world." He sounded really serious too. Though I didn't know whether he meant basketball was helping Win, or just that I was getting him out of himself for a while.

26

GETTING TO KNOW THE NEW NORMAL

AFTER OUR DAILY SUPER FUN MORNING WORKOUTS, I'd need a shower and Win would need a nap because he was so worn out from yelling at me. Then a couple hours later he'd wake up all raring to go to the daily beehive of therapy.

Physical therapy meant lots of stretching so his body wouldn't curl up, and electric stim to all sorts of muscles, from his quads to his hands, so they'd be ready to work when and if the nerves ever decided to reconnect. Some of the muscles already were working, like when he moved his toes, but other ones only worked sometimes depending on how fresh he was, or other factors no one could figure out due to the whole mystery of nerve regeneration. He'd lift weights — three pounds, or five pounds, which was a huge deal when he got to that. And very soon — too soon, I thought — they had him hanging in a big harness so he could practice walking movements, to get *those* muscles going and to work on balance, which is another huge thing for SCI.

It could have been really depressing considering what he

used to lift and how fast he used to run, but no one brought that up, not even Win. The nurses just said how lucky he was to have all this strength coming in, like his whole football career had been preseason training for SCI. And Dennis spent a lot of time in the PT department cheering him on. That was his job actually. The hospital folks, not being stupid, paid him real money to encourage PT patients, and he also drove a delivery truck, which is just as amazing.

The whole time Win was being worked on, he'd be on my case about *my* PT, yakking about my form so much that I had a little pang of guilt at how I'd yakked at Brian all summer. Although Win wasn't the only one who'd lost muscle mass. When he called me flabby—which I remember like it was burned in my ears, thank you very much—he meant my muscles looked like they hadn't been used in a while, which they hadn't been thanks to him. And I have to say that it felt pretty good to get them back into action. Plus those goofy PT lifts the doctors recommended really did seem to help my shoulder.

Then we'd go to OT. The occupational therapy room has a little pretend house all set up with a working kitchen and bathroom, even one of those little tables for changing babies' diapers, and a huge part of OT is just learning how to get around this house. Loading the dishwasher for example, if you have hands enough for that job (which Win did after a while, ha, even though he'd never once loaded it at home), or navigate with an electric wheelchair even if nothing on your body worked except your mouth. OT means learning how to help someone transfer you (or transfer yourself if you can) from a bed to a chair or a chair to a car, to dress yourself, to brush your teeth. To eat. Which Win did as well, and watching him shovel in meatloaf with a spoon strapped to his wrist made me just as proud and excited as watching him score a touchdown. Even Win let his guard down enough to smile, although it wasn't a big secret to anyone in the hospital how much he hated having other people feed him. He was even letting me feed him now, without any silent treatment, in the cafeteria.

By the time Win finished therapy he'd be shaking all over, so tired he was like a rag doll, and it took three of us to get him into bed so he could sleep for a bunch of hours. The nurses swore this was normal, and really good, especially considering how hard he was pushing himself. They were constantly reminding him not to overexert, and then boosting him, and me too, when things seemed to slide and he couldn't do what he'd done the day before. That was normal. Everything was normal. Not a normal I'd ever seen, but normal here in this hospital.

Sometimes Win and I would just talk. Like once he was getting stretched by Maryann who'd gotten him that whistle — she'd played basketball in college — and he said, grunting at the stretch, which Maryann said was a good sign because it showed he was feeling it, "So who's this guy?"

"What guy?" I asked.

"This guy from *Hawley*."

"It was nothing," I said, wishing I were smart enough to change the subject.

"Was that the guy in the article?" Maryann asked. "He sure didn't look like nothing."

Which made me feel even better, you can be sure.

"Are you sleeping together?" Win asked.

"Win!" For one thing, you don't talk like that, not if you're a Schwenk, and you sure don't talk like that in front of a *stranger*, even if she is a physical therapist. "No!"

"Oh, come on!" Maryann said. She grinned at Win. "I mean, if he asked nicely . . ."

"Did he ask you nicely?" Win asked me, grinning himself.

"No! Jeepers . . ." In the end, I told them the whole story, how Brian came by the farm to help, which made Win raise his eyebrows, and the turkey farmers who turned out to be reporters, which made them both just about fall over laughing if Win could fall over, and how Brian was two different people when he was alone with me and when he was in public, and how I figured out he was embarrassed about me. It hurt to talk about it, especially that I embarrassed him, but the fact I could even say this stuff out loud showed the hurt was going away a bit. I think.

"Oh, I'm sorry about that," said Maryann.

"He's not quarterback material," Win sniffed, like this was the biggest insult ever.

"Why do you say that?" she asked.

"Because he's not a leader. If he can't get those guys to respect his girlfriend, how's he going to lead them on the field?"

Maryann nodded. "Oh. I thought you were going to say a real quarterback wouldn't diss someone as great as D.J."

I blushed, but Win frowned in his football coach way. "You're probably right about that."

Win and I talked a lot, actually. At night I'd do his range of motion work, or help him with the ones he could do himself—all these specific exercises to keep him flexible. Keeping his joints moving was pretty critical, especially because a tiny bit more feeling and control was coming every couple days to different parts of his body. I had to do each exercise ten times and there were about two dozen exercises, so the whole thing took a while. We talked about the family, Dad's big dreams about going organic, the whole cheese business that made Win laugh. Especially when I asked who'd want to buy handmade cheese once they'd seen Dad's hands. Although Win didn't think it was such a bad idea. He'd done a project on organic farming in one of his business classes and said there really could be some money in it.

We even talked a bit about the Fight, and how Win never even wanted the farm and had wished his whole life Dad would change his mind.

"Well, at least you won't be stuck with it now," I said. Which wasn't so nice to point out, I realized as soon as I'd said it, but Win just laughed.

He looked at me. "It really should go to you, you know."

I snorted. "That's a real brilliant idea."

"You're the best damn farmer I've ever seen," he said in that don't-argue voice he's got. "A helluva lot better than Dad."

Which was something to think about, you can be sure.

And we talked about Curtis. Win couldn't believe Curtis had a girlfriend, and he busted a gut about Curtis and the science fair, once he stopped sputtering about Curtis joy riding illegally and cutting school, and he made that barf/curious face about the rats. He was really tickled that Curtis and Sarah had done so well, and said it was about time one of us did more than just run around.

With all the workouts Win was putting me through, and the rest of the time I spent being his slave, or doing all the homework I was forever trying to catch up on, I'd crawl into bed at nine o'clock each night just delighted to go to sleep. Maybe Win still had his midnight crying jags, but I sure didn't have the energy to stay awake and find out, or the courage to ask him. But I don't think he did. I felt so much better, in my brain as well as my shoulder, which by now was so strong that I could shoot almost anything. Having Win back—back emotionally, and ready to fight for his recovery the same way he'd always fought for football—that was a relief like you can't even imagine. Like a two-hundred-pound weight had been lifted off my heart. Mom said she was improving as well. She and I talked every day, and she had long conversations with Win and was just so happy about him that I know he was healing her back more than any medicine or the stretching she was doing. She'd been working from home ever since she'd slipped that disk, having people stand in for her as principal (seeing as she couldn't stand, ha) at the elementary school. Now, though, she was going to take an official leave of absence, once Dr. Miller said she was up for it, so she could come to Win. And she and Kathy Ott were trying to figure out how to come over with Curtis for just for a day or two before then, which depended on Mom's back and whether she could manage the ride. That was great, thinking about them visiting.

I thought about Brian a lot still, but not with quite as much hurting. I missed him so much, but I had to keep reminding myself that I didn't miss all of Brian, I just missed part of him, the part that was okay with being my friend. And sometimes I'd have to tell myself, like I was Win giving a lecture or something, that I was worth more than half a guy. But all in all I was too busy to spend too much time thinking about romance.

I guess I was alone on that one, though.

See, the one thing Win wouldn't let me help him with was

showering. Which of course is another thing you have to practice because a shower becomes a whole new experience in a wheelchair. Win's room had a bathroom all set up with a special shower chair and handholds, and that's where you had to practice taking a shower. But Win wouldn't let me go in with him even though I'd seen a lot more of him these past weeks than I ever wanted. He went with a PT instead, and then the next time he did as well, and because I was so busy trying to recover from his coaching, it took me a while to notice that that PT was always Maryann.

Then one day Maryann pointed out that I deserved a vacation—which I did. And from the way Win perked up, I finally got suspicious that maybe Win had ideas about Maryann that weren't totally, you know, therapy-related. And from the way Maryann smiled when he looked at her, maybe she had the same kind of ideas. Then Win gave this huge gasp, so huge that I thought something was wrong. But it turns out he was just disgusted with himself because he had only now remembered that I really needed to visit some universities and talk to coaches about their programs, like the one thing he should have been thinking about for the past month was how to promote my future in college basketball.

He made me call Bill right away. We'd talked to Bill a lot, almost every day, but this time he started ordering Bill to set up an appointment with the University of Minnesota b-ball coach, and make sure it wasn't a recruitment blackout or anything so I wouldn't violate any NCAA rules, and make sure to get me there for a game as well, and do all of this immediately, and finally Win looked at me in total disgust and said, "You talk to him."

Just taking the phone headset off Win's head, I could hear Bill sobbing.

"Hey," I said, "it's okay—"

"It's amazing," Bill gasped out, laughing and crying at the same time. "He's the same son of a bitch he always was."

Then Win called Charlie Wright and said he was ready. Because Charlie had been begging to come east and help, he'd had a couple conversations with the Packers coach, telling him how hard Win was working and how much Win wanted that Packers job. So when Win said he wanted me to have a little break, Charlie just about climbed right through the phone line and said he'd be there ASAP. Which meant the next day, which is pretty ASAP if you ask me, and Bill showed up to take me to Minneapolis.

27

BIG TRIP #2

IF YOU'RE THINKING that a lot sure has happened since D.J.'s last trip, and that this trip might be a little bit different, then you would be totally right. For one thing, this time I rode with Bill and Aaron because it's Aaron's car as always, Aaron telling me what a great girl I was and that if Bill ever gave me any grief I should tell him so he could smack Bill around.

"Although," he said, really serious, "I'd have to be careful not to damage my hands."

Which made me just crack up because it's such a funny image of *anyone* smacking Bill around. Though Aaron is so huge that he probably could. He makes Bill look small, even, and whenever he's next to me I feel like a normal-size girl instead of a giant, which I like a lot, that feeling. Also, Aaron and Bill are such good friends that I don't think they've gotten into an argument ever, so smacking around is kind of impossible.

Minneapolis looked like a science fiction movie, all these shiny skyscrapers, and the U of M campus was just so

campuslike, with sidewalks and grass, and pretty old build-
ings and fancy new ones, and some ugly ones too, to balance
it out. Bill even walked me to my big talk thing with the girls'
basketball program. Only in college it's called *women's* basketball, which makes it sound like they sit at a table discussing global finance or something.

An assistant coach—college sports have as many coaches
as players, it seems—showed me around all the sports build-
ings and didn't get lost once, and asked lots of questions. She
already knew about my playing football, and that I was taking care of Win, which seemed to impress her a lot, and she
seemed even more impressed about the training schedule
Win and I had worked out. She even seemed to understand
about my missing sophomore-year b-ball, and she gave me
lots of advice on what I needed to do to get recruited, how I
needed to play summer ball to get the coaches' attention.
Which I knew already, but who has time on a farm for basketball camp and traveling teams? She made it clear, though,
that this was pretty important, and I decided that when the
time came I'd have her talk to Dad about getting me off farm
work.

I really wanted to practice with the team, but that is one
of the five gazillion violations of NCAA rules, so I just
watched instead. Holy cow. I mean, I'm the best girls' basketball player in Red Bend, probably the best in our league,
but those girls are *good*. The whole time when I wasn't thinking Wow, or How did she do that, I was taking all these men-

tal notes on stuff I had to work on, which was pretty much everything. Except foul shots. I've got those down at least.

Maybe the coach told them to or maybe they're just automatically nice, but during one of their water breaks a couple girls came over to chat. One of them who had lots of little straight braids pulled back in a huge ponytail asked what "D.J." meant.

"Darlene Joyce," I said, rolling my eyes. "My two grandmothers. It's really dumb."

"Is it as dumb as Tyrona? 'Ty-ro-na, Ty-ron-*ah*.' It's like they get pregnant and all the blood drains right out of their brains. You know what I'm saying?" Then she invited me to dinner, in a real college dining hall.

Tyrona's a sociology major, which means studying what's wrong with people using numbers. At least that's how I understood it. Another thing about Tyrona is that she sure can put it away, although the other players aren't such picky eaters either, which I loved.

They had a ton of questions about Win, of course, and one of them knew a kid in school with SCI so she had a lot to say. Then Tyrona wanted to know about football and she wouldn't stop until I'd told the entire story, pretty much every detail including Brian, and she just ate it up.

"What are we doing here?" she asked the other girls. "We could be out there breaking new ground, and we're just shooting hoops."

"I'm not breaking ground now," I pointed out.

"Of course you're not—it's November, woman. The ground is *frozen*. You wanna go out?"

That too was quite the experience, seeing Tyrona's room and her signed posters of all the WNBA teams and players, and she dressed me because of course I hadn't brought any going-out clothes, or owned any really, and I sure don't have money to waste on stuff like that. But that's one nice thing about hanging out with Division I women's basketball players: they're all pretty much my size. We went to a party with music I'd never heard before but I liked it, and just as we walked in, Aaron gave this huge whoop because he was there too, and he grabbed me and said, "Hey, y'all, this is Milkshake's baby sister so you all be nice to her." Which is how I learned that Bill's nickname is Milkshake, which he had never felt the need to mention.

I also learned that Aaron's nickname is Tink, short for Tinkerbell, which he is pretty much the opposite of. Although he might have gotten it for another reason, because—and I know this is a huge stereotype about black people, I'm well aware of that—but that guy can *dance*. I mean, he's around 320, but on the dance floor he must have magic slippers or something—it's like he weighs twenty pounds max. Which really impressed me, especially seeing as us Wisconsin folks aren't really known for our, you know, dancing ability, but he took me under his wing and got me dancing too, or at least relaxed enough that I wasn't seizing up from terror at how bad I looked.

If I ever coach football, which is a long shot I know, the very first thing I'm going to do is hire Aaron to come teach all the players to dance, because anyone who can move like that would be pretty much unstoppable.

Bill was there as well, hanging out as always in a big cloud of girls, which would have bummed me out if I wasn't getting so much attention from Aaron on my dancing and stuff. I mean, at times I've been kind of jealous of Bill's abilities to make friends and girlfriends so easily. Not that I want girlfriends but you understand. If I'd been there alone, without Aaron and Tyrona making me feel welcome, I'd be sitting in a corner getting sad about Brian.

But here's the thing: it felt so different here, away from Red Bend and all that high school social stuff. Back in Red Bend, I would never get invited to a party like this — I almost never got invited to parties, period. And these were cool people. I mean, I don't know how they fit into the whole U of M pecking order — I'm sure there were kids somewhere on campus who would look at this party as uncool or unhip or something. But I didn't care, and I got the sense that no one else there cared either. They were having a good time with people they liked, and that's all that mattered to them.

Maybe that's what college is. Maybe it's that town full of strangers I'd been hoping to find with Brian. It's a place where you can start new without anyone sticking their noses in the air about your growing up on a dairy farm or being taller than almost all the boys in school, or having gay friends. Maybe the people at this party acted like that back in high school, I don't know. I didn't know them then. But maybe they'd grown up enough not to be like that anymore.

Brian — maybe he'll grow up too, in his town full of strangers wherever he goes to college. But at the moment I didn't care too much about his growing up, because I felt — this is going to sound pretty stuck up, I'm sure — but I felt that by the time he did, I'd be too grown up to care. Or maybe I was already. Besides, dancing was too much fun to think about people like Brian.

We left the party pretty early, actually, because Bill and Aaron were still on football time and had a curfew, which was fine with me. Aaron crashed with a friend down the hall so I could have his bed, which was huge just like him. The next morning I slept in for the first time in years, which felt like absolute heaven, and I walked around campus for the rest of the day pretending I was a real college student. That was a pretty heady feeling, let me tell you. Although it didn't compare one tiny iota to that night when I got to go to a women's basketball exhibition game. *Wow.* Almost ten thousand people — ten thousand! — watched, and they were extremely loud, and the game was extremely amazing, and Minnesota won because they've got a total home-court advantage, and I couldn't help but think that however exciting Red Bend football had been, this was a totally different league.

Afterward Bill took me back to his room because he actually had to study, which I guess is part of college too, and I didn't mind one bit seeing as I had my own homework to do. And then the next morning he drove me back to the rehab hospital. Back to reality. Although I felt so great, it was like I'd been gone three months instead of just two nights. And we didn't even stop at the Mall of America though it was right there with huge signs begging us to come in. We just drove right past it.

As happy as I was to be at U of M, I think Win was twice as happy to have three days with Charlie Wright, talking football around the clock while Charlie helped him. Charlie had even brought some Packers tapes. Win still couldn't watch live TV football for reasons I'm sure you can understand, but this was a *job,* which of course Win was totally into, and he and Charlie pored over them, talking all sorts of stuff that would probably have bored even me.

Bill came up to visit for a bit and join in all the football talk, stuff about pro ball that I'd never even imagined, it's so far from Red Bend. Although I did get to point out that if Bill ever got drafted, he'd either be training under Win or playing against him, both of which would pretty much suck. Which made them all crack up, even though Win had to add that *maybe* he'd get that assistant's position, and of course *maybe* Bill would be good enough for the NFL. Thanks, Win.

Then Charlie said, in a voice like they'd been through this before, "You need a degree before they'll hire you." What is it with grownups and college degrees?

Win stiffened, if you can stiffen in a cervical cream-cheese collar. "I know that!"

I had no idea what they were talking about but I sure didn't want to set Win off, and Bill must have felt the same way because right away he started talking about this girl he'd met who had eyes that are two different colors. Which wasn't the most exciting way to change the subject but it sure beat irritating Win.

Later when Win was napping, Charlie explained that the University of Washington would still give Win a full scholarship, which was awfully nice of them considering that he'd ruined his life playing for them although I don't mean to sound bitter. But of course in order to get that degree, Win would have to go back to school. With assistants if he needed them, specially trained people so it's not all dumped on your family. And Charlie said that folks at the university, and folks in Red Bend too, like Kathy Ott and Cindy Jorgensen, who apparently are angels from heaven sent to care for us Schwenks, were organizing fundraisers and stuff because SCI costs so much. Wheelchairs cost a ton, even the manual ones and don't ask about electric, and rebuilding bathrooms and kitchens—which our house will need, duh—and those specially trained aides, and PT, and a whole bunch of other stuff. So the fact that people out there wanted to give money to Win was awfully nice.

Which brought up what Charlie and Win had been fighting about, that Win wanted the degree but he didn't want to go to class with the other students. And even though he liked the idea of fundraising, he refused to talk about something like a press conference, which of course would be the best way to get the word out. Even when Charlie said that Win needed to be a role model, which usually works on him the way the words "free beer" work on Bill, Win objected. He didn't want people looking at him and talking about him and feeling sorry for him. Which I could understand, but I could understand Charlie's point too.

Anyway, we talked about this a while, and when Win woke up he transferred to the wheelchair with not too much help from me and Charlie, showing Bill how good he was getting, and I wheeled him downstairs to say goodbye. Charlie asked Win to come out to the curb where his rental car was but Win wouldn't. He said it was because it was too cold, but it was clear to all of us that Win didn't want to be out in public, on a street where he could be seen by strangers. So that was a bit of an awkward moment, and then Charlie and Bill both hugged us and said how impressed they were by Win's progress, and off they went while I took Win back upstairs.

I thought about pointing out that hiding inside wasn't how captains acted, but I didn't because I'm not that stupid.

28

DAY OF THANKS

EVERYONE WAS TALKING ABOUT WIN actually going home for Thanksgiving. Which really is kind of a miracle, a Grandpa Warren hard-work miracle, not the God-is-easy-on-you kind. We had a couple big phone calls with Mom and Dad, organizing a trip back to Schwenk Farm just for Thanksgiving Day, not spending the night because that's months away yet. Maryann even volunteered to go with us to assess the house — that's something they do with every patient although usually not on Thanksgiving, which makes me think that Maryann was making, you know, a special exception. Then again, her family's in Nebraska and maybe she didn't have anything else to do, who knows.

A few days before Thanksgiving, Win got a head cold and I thought that was it. But he recovered before it went into his chest, which would be really bad because the whole pneumonia thing with quads, and now it looked like we were really good to go. Win even had these ceramic turkey candleholders he'd made in art class that Mom would just bawl her head off over.

Wednesday afternoon Dad showed up to stay the night then drive us back, Win and Maryann and me. We kept saying this wasn't necessary, that in fact it was an extremely bad idea because Win needs a special van — he can't just be wheeled onto the pickup bed. But Dad insisted. Then when he showed up, I could see why.

He was driving a new van. I mean, brand new. It was so new it didn't have a license plate even, just a paper form. And a wheelchair lift and everything. Dad climbed out of that van like it was his fifth child. He'd called from the road to make sure I'd be out front when he pulled up.

"That's not ours," I said.

"Oh yeah it is. Just got it." He patted the shiny new paint. It's been a long time since he had a shiny ride. "All we pay for is gas."

"But who — where —"

"That fellow of yours? Well, his father started up a collection with truck dealers, all over Wisconsin I think, and they pooled up and got this."

"*Brian's* father? The one who almost sued the school about me?"

Dad nodded. He looked as surprised as I did, and he'd had time to absorb it. "You just can't tell about some people." He started to cry. "You can't tell what's inside them."

Which I had to agree with, though I didn't have any time to chew this over because Dad right away wanted to see Win, and he started crying even more watching Win wheel himself over to shake his hand. That got the nurses going even. Win showed Dad all over the hospital, me pushing most of the time because he can't wheel for long and it's not so good for his shoulders. Win was pretty much head honcho these days, speaking to new patients, busting guys who weren't working as hard as he thought they should be, joking around with Dennis, who nearly gave Dad a heart attack when he came rushing over to greet him. There was a huge duffel of Win's medical stuff, all these things he'd need and stuff we sure hoped he wouldn't, and I was extremely glad Maryann was coming because there was no way I could have handled that by myself. I couldn't even *identify* most of it.

Dad spent the night with me in the little apartment, and I got to make him French toast for dinner, really late, because that's the only thing I know how to cook, Dad drinking beer, which normally doesn't go with French toast but guess how much he cared.

"You know, I saw Brian," Dad said after a while.

I shrugged, but inside my stomach flipped. I tried to think of what to say: "Oh" . . . "We broke up" . . . "Did he talk about me?" But I couldn't think of anything, not without a couple weeks' effort.

"He came by with his dad to drop off the van. Asked me to say hello."

"Oh," I managed to get out at last. "That's—that's nice."

"It is. He's had an easy life, that boy has." There was a long silence, and then Dad held up a forkful of French toast. "You didn't use any cinnamon, I see."

I had to grin. "Couldn't find any."

"Well, they taste perfect like this. Just perfect." He clinked his beer against my glass of milk, and the conversation drifted over to Curtis, how Dad had just about lost his teeth, the fake ones, the first time he saw those rats.

Walking into Win's room the next morning, though, I could tell something was wrong. Just the way he sat staring out the window made me think, Uh-oh.

"Hey there, ready to hit the road?" I said, hoping to bluff my way through.

"I'm not going," Win said flatly.

"So, we've got a van, we've got a therapist — the prettiest therapist, which is nice — we've got Dad ready to pull out a handkerchief for just about anything. We've got the turkey candlesticks. Anything we're missing?"

"I'm not going."

I sat down on the edge of the bed. "Okay."

"People know me here. They know what I look like."

"So you're saying you don't want to go for Thanksgiving, or you don't want to go, period?"

Win didn't answer.

"Because you're going to have to leave the building eventually. They'll kick you out."

"Do you know what people will say, seeing me?" he asked bitterly, gesturing to his wheelchair. "'Oh, look at that crippled guy. Isn't that sad. Isn't he brave.' I *hate* that garbage. I hate it."

That lingered there in the hospital room for a few minutes, those words.

I swallowed. "We've got a little brother," I said, kind of out of the blue, "who's really smart. Which, you know, is not something that comes naturally to us. He's probably going to go to med school or something. And he made this thing — with rats, but still — and it won a huge prize. But he couldn't tell anyone. He got in so much trouble, and so did Sarah, because everyone thought they were fooling around. But having people think *that*, that was easier for the two of them than the truth. The truth that they're smart."

Win didn't say anything, but he was listening.

"And I used to have a boyfriend. Who actually is a really nice guy, and his dad got us that van, which is pretty amazing. But we broke up because he couldn't stand what his friends might think. I might not be the best girl in the world, or the prettiest —"

"You're both those things," said Win.

"Prettier than Maryann?"

"Shut up. Keep talking."

"Anyway, we broke up because he was afraid of what his friends said. And that's kind of pathetic, I think." I sighed. "I have another friend, a *real* friend. She said once — just a couple weeks ago, actually—that you can't control what people say about you. And she should know."

"Was this Amber?"

(I'd told Win about Amber too, which I thought would be a huge revelation but he just laughed and asked me if I'd ever been in a weight room. Whatever that means.)

"Nah, her girlfriend."

Win thought for a moment. "'You can't control what people say about you' . . . She's got a smart girlfriend."

"Yeah, she does."

"So are you going to help me out of here?"

"I suppose so," I said, giving him a punch in the arm. Not too hard, but hard enough. Hard enough to let him know he couldn't be broken.

So that was the beginning of our big trip home for Thanksgiving, and it would have been the emotional high point probably, if we hadn't driven through Hawley.

Okay, I know I haven't mentioned much about Red Bend football lately, but it turns out Red Bend and Hawley finished the season tied for first, and they were playing each other for the league championship. This was the big Thanksgiving Day game everyone goes to every year.

Which Dad knew, even though he also wasn't paying as much attention as he usually does. So while we were on the road, Dad asked if it was okay if we drove through Hawley. He didn't even mention the game, just said that Jimmy Ott wanted to wave. Which Jimmy did want to do. He'd been so much a part of our family, he and Kathy, that he really wanted, you know, just to acknowledge Win as we drove by, step out of his office before the game started to do that. And so Dad called from his cell phone — oh, Dad has a cell phone now, did I forget to mention that? So he can call the cows in for milking, ha ha — Dad called Jimmy to let him know we'd be passing by.

Anyway, we ended up leaving the hospital a lot later than we'd planned because everything takes so much longer with, well, with everything, and so Dad's big plan to pass through Hawley two hours before the game got all screwed up, and instead he called about fifteen minutes before kickoff when Jimmy was in the middle of his locker room pep talk. And because Jimmy is such a loyal, wonderful person, and also because he thought it might really inspire his players, he made the whole Hawley team come out to the street with him. And when Jeff Peterson heard what was going on, then of course he had to bring the Red Bend players out as well, seeing as he was one of Win's coaches back in high school. And then the cheerleaders joined in because that's what they do, and a whole bunch of Red Bend fans went racing for the gates — especially because Kathy had organized a fund drive for Win before the game, with ladies at every gate collecting money in Red Bend football helmets, which sort of put Win on everyone's minds . . .

But we didn't know any of this. Even Dad and Jimmy Ott weren't expecting this. So Dad looked just as surprised as the rest of us in the van when we turned onto the street that runs past the high school and there, all of a sudden, was everyone. All these people lining the road, both sides, and cheerleaders too, and Beaner yelling his head off and jumping up and down, and all the Hawley players, probably Brian even, though I couldn't make him out in that blur of orange uniforms—

They were there for us. For Win. It was like a parade, only he was the only person in it. He sat in the van in his wheelchair looking out at all this, and Maryann leaned over and whispered, "You gotta wave," and she was crying, and I was crying, and the people outside had huge tears running down their faces as they smiled away, and I realized with a start that not being able to control what people say about you sometimes includes their good words too. And Win waved to them with his weak-triceps wave, and they cheered even more because Win is the best football player Red Bend has ever produced, and nothing that happens to him can ever change that.

When we made it to the farm finally, I had another surprise, because Amber and Dale had come back from Chicago to help Mom with dinner. Which Mom kept secret just to see the look on my face. Actually, Amber and her mom were

talking again. Lori had come over to cut Mom's hair and after hearing all about Win's problems decided that maybe
having a gay kid isn't so bad considering she can still walk.
Lori was supposed to come too, but she was late because of
her new boyfriend, which surprised no one and didn't bother
anyone either.

Guess what Dale made for dinner.

Actually, she and Dad hit it off like gangbusters, which
I should have figured out if I'd thought about it for even a
second. Whether Dad knows about her and Amber I don't
know—sometimes the not-talking thing works out just
fine—and he and Dale spent a couple hours outside with
beers and her barbecue machine gabbing away about season-
ings. She got him all fired up again about organic cheese and
said she'd build him a smokehouse even, so that he came
back into the kitchen looking like he'd just met Santa.

I went searching and finally found Curtis's science fair trophy stuffed in the back of his closet. I brought it back downstairs, Curtis scuttling over to grab it but I wouldn't let him
because it's the first trophy any Schwenk ever won for brains.
It actually got pretty rough and I had to use some basketball
moves that are illegal, but I insisted we keep it right on the
dining room table, next to Win's candlesticks. And I made
Curtis tell Maryann and Kathy and Jimmy Ott all about it,
Kathy so proud that she cried a little even though rats give
her nightmares.

This whole time Mom looked so happy to have Win home finally, and she fluttered around him beaming like her face was going to split in two. She'd spent days getting the house ready, and she'd cleaned out the little office — or made Dad and Curtis clean it — and even got a hospital bed in there somehow so Win could take a nap after that huge exhausting trip. Which he actually did, and her being able to help him like that, you could tell it took away a big chunk of her pain about not being with him in the hospital. She spent a lot of time with Maryann too, showing her around and talking about Win. And Smut, even though she's got tons of enthusiasm most of the time, she crawled up on Win's hospital bed as gently as she ever could, and nestled down next to him like she knew with her good-dog sense that he was hurt, and stayed curled up with him for his entire nap, looking so proud to be there for her man like that.

Right as we were finally sitting down to dinner, Bill and Aaron — or Milkshake and Tink if you want to be that way — showed up, even though Bill had told us he didn't think he'd be able to make it back in time. They'd ducked out of their football game the second it finished so they could race over here. And we all sat down to the best food I have ever eaten, especially compared to all that hospital food these past months, and more than that to the best people I know, and we all bowed our heads in thanks. Even Win.

29

Easy Lives

After dinner we got Win all packed up and he and Maryann and Mom headed back to Minnesota. Even Dr. Miller
said Mom was good enough to go so long as she doesn't try
lifting him. I get to stick around in Red Bend with Dad and
Curtis, for a while it looks like, as the female head of household, which is a term that always cracks me up because there
isn't a household I know that isn't headed by a female, and
most of the males in those households wouldn't last two
minutes if it was the other way around.

Which meant that the first job I got stuck with as female
head of household was cleaning up Thanksgiving dinner,
only it turned out to be a blast with me and Amber and Dale
and Kathy Ott laughing our heads off, even Kathy dancing to
this CD Dale had brought—Melissa somebody—while
Amber lip-synched the songs. And Aaron went out to help
Bill and Dad and Curtis milk, only he had *them* laughing so
hard it's a wonder they got a drop out of those cows.

They all stayed around for a while, playing cards and picking at the leftover pieces of barbecued turkey even though

everyone was so full. I didn't say much because I was thinking about how happy Mom looked behind the wheel of that new van, getting to drive her son, and I got this idea and before I lost my nerve I went into the little office and called the Nelsons. Not Brian's cell phone. Their house.

The phone rang a couple times while I got second thoughts. What do you say to a man you've never met who never liked you too much and still does something as amazing as that van? Does "thank you" cut it? Maybe I should write instead, like I'm any good at that either —

"Happy T-Day," Brian answered, sounding pretty pleased with life.

"Hey. Um, it's —"

"D.J.?" I guess it's pretty easy to identify me on the phone.

"Yeah. Hey, Brian . . . I just wanted to call and thank your dad for that van. And, you know, wish you folks a happy Thanksgiving."

"Oh. Don't mention it."

"No, that van — that's the most generous thing I've ever seen in my life. Really."

"Well, it meant a lot. He got more satisfaction from that, jeez, than anything I can remember."

I couldn't think of a thing to say. Now I really regretted calling. I'm sure it looked like I did it just to talk to Brian. And I guess that secretly I did want to talk to him, but using the van like that made me look pretty pathetic —

"So, you're back in town?" Brian asked.

"Uh, looks that way. I'll be doing basketball and everything."

"Boys' or girls'?" he asked, grinning a little—you could hear it.

"I dunno. I have to check out the Hawley teams, see which one is, you know, good enough for me to play against." We both laughed, and for a moment it felt like it used to. Like it should.

"Listen . . ." Brian began, and I knew what was coming. The apologies, the explanations. Solutions he'd thought up that wouldn't work, not in Wisconsin, anyway.

"Don't," I said. "Please. You take care, okay?"

"You too," he said, and I held on to that phone, wishing there was something else to say, but I guess there wasn't because after a while I heard the click of Brian hanging up, and I did too, and I went back to this poker game Dale had organized with Bill and Aaron and the Otts, Dad insisting that red queens were always wild, which Amber backed him up on—the first time in my life that's happened, Amber and Dad on the same side of a discussion.

Last summer I had to write this huge English paper about why I wanted to play football—write because of flunking sophomore English and everything—and that paper was supposed to be my official makeup project. Anyway, it turned out that it really helped me figure out a bunch of stuff that was going on in my life. And Mrs. Stolze said some awfully nice things about it, which doesn't happen too often, getting praise from English teachers. She's the one who gave me the idea to put down everything that's happened this fall. She says it's like having a baby: you think you'll remember every detail and then all of a sudden that baby is grown up and everything went too fast.

It turns out she's right. These months have been one thing after another, and yet if I hadn't written it all down, I'd barely remember the details, all the awful stuff. Besides, these days I'm too busy thinking about basketball, and school, and Amber, who's talking about coming back to finish her senior year and Dale's encouraging her, telling her to stick it out with her mom. Plus I've got to teach Curtis to be proud of his brains, help him find new friends if he has to because kids who make fun of you aren't really your friends. And you know what? After all that trauma and drama and pain, Win is going to survive. He's going to be better than he ever was, if you want to know the truth. Because the one thing he never was was humble.

I keep thinking about what Dad said over French toast, that night he came to the rehab hospital in the van. He said Brian had an easy life. I mean, Brian's handsome and rich, and he's always been popular, and he gets along with almost everyone and he knows how to talk about things that we Schwenks couldn't manage without being cattle-prodded.

And he's probably the smartest kid in his school. But I don't think that's what Dad was talking about. Dad hasn't had an easy life. He got stuck with the farm when there was no one else to run it, and he's had to watch it bleed away money—I still don't know if it's going to make it, though I'm keeping my fingers crossed that we'll come up with something, Dad and me, some way to get folks to buy Schwenk milk instead of that cow-factory stuff. Plus Dad's hip pained him all those years until he finally got it replaced, and now Win being hurt—that's tough. And he knows how hard my life has been too—not just farm work but that I'm not so good at school, and I've never had many friends or even a boyfriend until Brian. I don't know how much Dad knows about what went on between the two of us, but I bet his theories aren't that far off.

But the thing is, Dad's not too fond of easy lives. Probably jealous, for one thing. But he's also seen how a tough life can make you stronger. It got Win and Bill all the way to college because they worked so hard at football. It got Win fighting for his survival. That's why Dad agreed to take Brian on last summer, because Jimmy Ott wanted Brian to get a work ethic and Schwenk Farm grows that better than anything. And Brian did learn how to work hard, and all season he started as QB thanks to us. But I guess he never learned those other kinds of toughness, like how to stand up to your so-called friends, and how to defend those people who really are your friends even if they're unpopular or poor or the wrong size. I think what Dad was saying that night—although I'm not sure because I'm never going to ask him—is that Brian's life has been too easy, and that maybe, just maybe, I deserve someone better. Someone else who's strong enough to take on a whole herd of trouble when it comes their way.

ACKNOWLEDGMENTS

Win's Minnesota hospital is a fictitious amalgam of the Model Spinal Cord Injury Centers, federally funded institutions throughout the United States that specialize in SCI rehabilitation and research. Magee Rehabilitation Hospital in Philadelphia is one such center; I will be forever grateful to Magee's Sarah Myer and Mary Schmidt Read, and the unlimited time, consideration, and enthusiasm they gave me.

My thanks to Adam Tagliaferra, Katrine Seghetti-Mayhew, Travis Roy, and the contributors to Richard Holicky's *Roll Models* for sharing their stories with the world. Doctors Marc McKenna and Garath Maenpaa, and physical therapists Drew Wallace and Brian Jerva, patiently answered my many strange and obscure inquiries. Patsey Kahmann and Becky Bohm at the University of Minnesota could not have been more hospitable.

Thanks as well to Hillary, Liz, Mari, Mimi R., Tracey, Uncles Nick and Rod, Mom, Dad, Dave, and the girls of Holton-Arms and Radnor Middle School for all your suggestions and hard truths. Jill Grinberg, my perfect agent, and Margaret Raymo, my perfect editor, had the great good sense to know when I needed to sulk, and to prod me when I needed to stop. Nick and Mimi listened closely and asked excellent questions. And thanks, most of all, to James, who first heard this story many moons ago and has bolstered me in more ways than he will ever know. Whatever courage I have, he gave me.